BATTLE OF THE ZOMBIES

BY THE BEASTLY BOYS

ILLUSTRATED BY JONNY DUDDLE

SIMON AND SCHUSTER

First published in Great Britain in 2010 by Simon & Schuster UK Ltd
A CBS COMPANY

This paperback edition published in 2012

1 3 5 7 9 10 8 6 4 2

Simon & Schuster UK Ltd
1st Floor
222 Gray's Inn Road
London
WC1X 8HB

www.simonandschuster.co.uk

Simon & Schuster Australia, Sydney
Simon & Schuster India, New Delhi

A CIP catalogue copy for this book is available
from the British Library.

ISBN: 978-0-85707-522-2

Printed and bound by CPI Group (UK) Ltd, Croydon, CR0 4YY

TONIGHT,
LOOK UP AT THE MOON.
LOOK AT IT CLOSELY.
STARE AT IT.
NOW ASK YOURSELF:
AM I FEELING
BRAVE?

BEASTLY
BUSINESS

CHAPTER ONE

It was the dead of night and high in the sky a hot-air balloon was drifting through the darkness. In its basket were three men. The tallest of them peered down through a telescope. 'We're approaching the target,' he said. 'Turn off the gas, Bone.'

'Yes, Baron Marackai,' a big man replied. He twisted a handle on the balloon's burner and its flame went out. The balloon began to slowly descend.

A small man gripped the basket, nervously sucking on a rag. 'I don't like the dark,' he said.

Baron Marackai turned, eyeing him. 'We don't want anyone seeing us, Blud, you idiot.

This is a secret mission, remember.' The Baron raised his right hand, wiggling a stump where his little finger was missing. 'Now, repeat after me: Death to the RSPCB.'

Blud and Bone quickly raised their right hands and turned down their little fingers. 'Death to the RSCPC,' they said.

'The RSPCB, you numbskulls.' The Baron swiped his telescope, clonking them on their noses. 'Now, silence. We're coming in to land.'

Blud and Bone peered over the side of the basket. The balloon was descending gently towards a large castle.

The balloon drifted slowly between towers and turrets then landed with a bump on the castle's rooftop.

The Baron stepped out on to the roof and looked down at the castle's outer walls where knights in armour were standing guard. 'Hah, the fools never saw us,' he muttered. 'Bone, hold the basket steady. We shall need it for our getaway. Blud, pass me the box.'

Blud and Bone climbed out. While Bone

held the basket, Blud handed the Baron a little wooden box.

Baron Marackai opened it and carefully took out two small bottles, one containing silver liquid and the other golden liquid. He grinned, watching them sparkle. 'This time the RSPCB is doomed.'

'What's the plan, Sir?' Blud whispered.

'Never you mind,' the Baron said. 'Just wait here and keep quiet.' Clutching the two bottles, he crept away across the rooftop and disappeared into the darkness.

Blud and Bone heard the rusty creak of a door opening, then the Baron's footsteps descending a flight of stone steps. They huddled together, hearing the wind whistling round the turrets and towers and strange moanings and groanings sounding from the castle's windows.

'What's he doing?' Blud asked.

Bone pointed to a walkway silhouetted between the main castle building and a tall tower. 'Look,' he whispered. The dark figure of

Baron Marackai was creeping along the walkway. There was a muffled clang then the Baron went inside the tower and a moment later reappeared with a second figure following him.

'Someone's with him,' Blud said. The two dark figures disappeared back into the main building, and Blud and Bone waited anxiously.

Suddenly, they heard shrieks and cries coming from inside the castle. Voices called out: 'It's incredible!'… 'Look at me!'… 'I'm alive!'

Then they heard footsteps running and Baron Marackai came hurrying back on to the rooftop, the second figure running alongside him. 'This way, Harold. We'll soon have you out of here,' the Baron said.

The Baron and his companion dashed to the hot-air balloon and jumped in its basket. 'Blud, Bone, get in,' the Baron ordered. 'It's time to go.'

Blud and Bone glanced at one another, puzzled, then climbed into the basket. Bone fired the burner and the balloon began to rise from the castle's roof up into the night sky.

The Baron picked a cobweb from his fur coat. 'Well, that all went rather well,' he said. 'Blud, Bone, I'd like you to meet Harold.'

Blud and Bone stared at the other man in the basket. The man had on a chainmail vest and a black leather tunic, but where his head should have been was just the stump of a neck. His head had been chopped off, and he was carrying it under his arm.

'Pleasssed to meet youuu,' the head hissed.

Blud and Bone gripped one another in terror.

'So, Harold, you're free at last,' the Baron said. 'Aren't you going to thank me for breaking you out?'

Harold held up his head to look the Baron in the eye. 'Thanksss,' it hissed.

The Baron grinned. 'That's quite all right, Harold. NOW, THERE'S SOMETHING I'D LIKE YOU TO DO FOR ME...'

CHAPTER TWO

It was a sunny morning at the Royal Society for the Prevention of Cruelty to Beasts, and Ulf was riding his quad bike across the Great Grazing Grounds towing a trailer full of smelly manure. He'd spent all morning in the meat-eaters' enclosure mucking out an Egyptian scorpius, a large venomous beast that was recovering from pincer-lock. Now he was on his way back across the beast park to drop the manure at the flower garden.

Ulf rode past Sunset Mountain and splashed on to the marsh where the bogwobbler was basking. He slowed his bike and from a canvas bag behind his seat he took out a bone and threw it to the beast. The bogwobbler's mouth opened like a crater in the mud, gobbling the bone whole.

Ulf sped on past Troll Crag then round the biodomes: enclosures for the extreme-weather beasts. He slowed alongside the snow dome where an ice dragon was recovering from a broken wing. Helping Hands – hand-shaped beasts that helped around the centre – were loading frozen fish into the dome's feeding cannon. They fired the fish and the ice dragon lurched, snatching the fish in its jaws. 'Good catch,' Ulf called.

As the ice dragon belched a jet of blue flames, Ulf smiled then twisted the bike's throttle with his hairy hand and accelerated away.

The RSPCB was a rescue centre for rare and endangered beasts, from washed-up sea monsters to vampires with toothache. Ulf was a beast himself, an orphaned werewolf, and had lived at the centre ever since he'd been brought in more than ten years earlier. He was now training to become an RSPCB agent.

Ulf rode into the lower paddock and saw Orson the giant wading in the freshwater lake.

'Morning, Orson,' Ulf called.

The giant glanced over. 'Morning, Ulf.'

Ulf pulled up beside the lake and saw that the giant was releasing a magnaturtle into the water. Orson handled all the large beasts. He let go of the amphibious emerald-shelled turtle and it flapped its flippers, gliding out across the lake like a floating island.

'Is it going to be all right now?' Ulf asked.

'Hopefully,' the giant replied. 'Dr Fielding operated on it. The poor thing had swallowed a plastic crate.'

Orson glanced at the manure in Ulf's trailer. He sniffed. 'Phwoar, that stuff smells 'orrible.'

'Does it? I suppose I've got used to it,' Ulf replied, smiling. He revved the bike's engine and sped away up the side of the paddock towards Farraway Hall, a large country house and the headquarters of the RSPCB.

He parked by the flower garden at the back of the house, then began unloading the manure with a shovel. Tall, thorny flowers scuttled over on their roots and wriggled into it. Ulf could hear them purring, then their petals opened red with delight. A sparkle darted up from them. It was Tiana the fairy, Ulf's best friend.

'Hey, watch out, Ulf! That stuff went on my new outfit!' she yelled, wiping her dress made from dried cornflowers.

'Sorry, Tiana,' Ulf said. 'I'm feeding the roving roses.'

The fairy sniffed. 'It stinks!'

'It's manure,' Ulf told her, throwing on another shovelful. 'It's scorpius poo – full of goodness, apparently.'

'Scorpius poo! You went in with the scorpius? You must be crazy.'

'It wasn't dangerous. I hypnotised it,' Ulf said. 'It says how to in *The Book of Beasts*.'

The Book of Beasts was Ulf's most precious possession, a notebook that had once belonged to Professor Farraway, the founder of the RSPCB, and it contained all kinds of tips and tricks on handling wild beasts.

Ulf leant on his shovel, listening to the roving roses slurp and burp as they fed.

Suddenly, he heard a loud trumpeting fanfare from the other side of Farraway Hall. 'What was that?' he said to Tiana. He looked around the side of the house and saw Dr Fielding, the RSPCB vet, rushing towards the forecourt.

'Something's going on,' Tiana said.

'Come on, let's take a look.' Ulf grabbed his bag from the quad bike and raced across the yard. He found Dr Fielding by the entrance gates, looking up the driveway. Galloping towards her was a unicorn and, riding on its back, was a knight in shining armour with a bugle in his hand.

'Woweee!' Tiana said, surprised.

Ulf watched, intrigued, as the knight pulled on the unicorn's reins and brought it to a standstill by the gates.

The knight raised the visor on his helmet and saluted to Dr Fielding. Ulf and Tiana both gasped; where the knight's face should have been was just hollow darkness. The knight's

helmet was empty, as if there was no one inside the suit of armour.

'Good morning,' Dr Fielding said to the knight. 'How can I help you?'

Without replying, the knight reached down through the bars of the gate and handed her a rolled-up paper scroll. Then he closed his visor and pulled on the unicorn's reins, turning it round. With a tap of his heels, the knight rode off back up the driveway.

'Who was that, Dr Fielding?' Ulf asked.

Dr Fielding was unrolling the paper scroll. 'That was a ghost knight, Ulf,' she replied.

'A ghost!' Tiana shrieked. She perched on Ulf's shoulder, trembling.

'There's no need to be frightened, Tiana,' Dr Fielding said. 'He was just delivering a message.'

Ulf stepped beside Dr Fielding and looked at the scroll:

TROUBLE AT HOWLHAMMER CASTLE.
COME QUICK!

'Howlhammer Castle? Where's that?' Ulf asked. He'd never heard of it before.

'It's about three hours north of here,' Dr Fielding explained. 'It's an RSPCB habitat for ghosts.'

'A *haunted* castle!'

'That's right, Ulf. **It's the most haunted place in the country.** Years ago, Professor Farraway declared it a site of special cryptozoological interest and had it protected by law.'

Ulf looked back at the scroll. 'What do you think the trouble is there?' he asked.

'Hmm, a phantom with a fever perhaps,' Dr Fielding replied. 'Or a poltergeist trapped in a cupboard, or maybe a ghoul with gas? Ghouls are always getting gas. We'd better drive up there and find out.' She rolled the scroll back up. 'Would you like to come? Howlhammer Castle has all kinds of ghosts to learn about. It would be good for your training.'

'I'd love to,' Ulf replied excitedly.

'Great. All RSPCB agents should know about ghosts, Ulf.' Dr Fielding turned to the fairy. 'And what about you, Tiana?'

'I… er… I… erm…'

Ulf could feel Tiana's wings fluttering nervously against his neck. 'Don't worry, Tiana, I'll look after you,' he whispered.

'Excellent,' Dr Fielding said. 'I'll radio Orson and fetch the truck. We'll leave in fifteen minutes.'

As she unclipped her walkie-talkie from her belt, she sniffed. 'What *is* that revolting smell?'

Tiana giggled. 'It's Ulf.'

Ulf looked at his hands, still mucky with manure. 'Don't worry, Dr Fielding. I promise to have a wash before we go.'

CHAPTER THREE

Ulf was washing his hands under the yard tap, thinking about the message the knight had brought in. He glanced down at Tiana, who was admiring the reflection of her new dress in a puddle. 'Tiana, the message on that scroll. It said "trouble".'

'So?'

The word TROUBLE worried Ulf. 'What if something bad's happened at Howlhammer?'

'Bad how?' the fairy asked.

'What if it's… Marackai?'

Tiana frowned. 'Oh Ulf, not this again. You've got to stop worrying about Marackai. When the pixies went missing you thought it was him and it turned out they were just hiding. When the frostbiters were poisoned you thought it was him and it turned out they'd just eaten grindleberries. Whenever anything is a bit out of the ordinary you think it's Marackai.' The fairy plucked a loose petal from the hem of her dress. 'Sometimes trouble just means normal trouble, Ulf.'

Ulf dried his hands on his T-shirt, still feeling unsettled. Marackai was Professor Farraway's son. He was mean and cruel to beasts and hunted them for fun. Four times Marackai had tried to destroy the RSPCB and four times Ulf had defeated him.

'Besides which,' Tiana said, smoothing her dress down, 'Marackai *must* be dead by now.'

The last time they'd seen Marackai, the beast hunter had been carried away in the claws of a vampire.

'I hope you're right, Tiana,' Ulf said. 'I hope he *is* dead.'

Just then, from above them, a gurgled voice started singing: 'Fur Face frightened. Run, run,

run! Marackai come with his big bad gun! Blurgh!'

Ulf looked up and saw Druce the gargoyle leering at him from a window-ledge. 'Morning, Druce,' Ulf said.

'Blurgh!' Druce replied, blowing a raspberry.

Tiana flew up to the gargoyle. 'Have you been eavesdropping, Druce?'

The gargoyle waggled his ears. 'Drucey hear everything,' he gurgled, then he flicked out his long tongue soaking the fairy in spit.

'Euch!' Tiana yelled. She blasted her sparkles back at him then chased him up a drainpipe to the rooftop.

Ulf smiled, seeing them play. Druce had lived on the rooftop ever since the house had been built, and he was always causing mischief. As Ulf watched the gargoyle bound along the guttering, a little light caught his eye at an upstairs window. A candle flame was flickering behind the glass. Professor Farraway? Ulf thought.

He stepped to the side door of the house and poked his head in. He could hear moaning and groaning coming from upstairs. 'Professor, is everything okay up there?' he called.

The moaning and groaning grew louder.

What Ulf knew, that Dr Fielding didn't, was that Professor Farraway was now a ghost too, and haunted upstairs at Farraway Hall.

Ulf glanced round, hearing the RSPCB truck drive into the yard. Orson was coming in from the beast park. Quickly, Ulf dashed into the house and sprinted upstairs. He saw the candle floating by a window at the end of the Gallery of Science. 'Professor, do you want something?' Ulf asked.

The candle began floating towards Ulf, moaning and groaning filling the corridor.

'Professor, what's the matter?'

The candle drifted past drawings and photographs on the corridor's walls, its light illuminating the pictures one after the other: a sketch of a minotaur's skull... a photograph of a goblin in its hole... an X-ray of a sphinx's brain... It stopped in front of a picture of a golden phoenix, and the picture began rattling on its hook. Ulf stepped nearer. 'Professor, is that you doing that?'

The picture rattled louder and Ulf felt the air turn cold. His skin began prickling with goose-bumps.

On the picture's glass he saw words appearing. An invisible finger was writing in the dust:

THE PRISONER IS MORE
DANGEROUS THAN YOU THINK

Ulf stared at the words, puzzled. 'Prisoner? What prisoner, Professor?'

Dust swirled up from the floor and Ulf felt the hairs on his neck stand on end as an icy chill whirled around him. 'Professor, I don't understand,' he said.

But the candle began drifting away down the corridor. Its flame flickered and it vanished into the gloom.

'Ulf, what are you doing here? Everyone's waiting,' he heard from the stairs. He saw Tiana hovering by the banister.

'I got held up,' Ulf told her. 'Look at this!'

The fairy flew over and saw the words on the dusty picture of the phoenix. 'What's all that?'

'The Professor wrote it,' Ulf told her. 'He called me up here.'

Tiana fluttered her wings impatiently. 'Well, it'll have to wait until we get back, Ulf. It's time to go.'

Outside, the truck's horn beeped.

'Come on. Quickly, Ulf.' The fairy zoomed back downstairs and Ulf followed her, still wondering what the Professor had meant.

The RSPCB truck was in the yard, its engine running. Orson was sitting in the back by a pile of equipment, and Druce was leaping up and down on the truck's roof.

'Oh no, is Druce coming too?' Tiana asked.

Orson smiled. 'Druce has got friends at Howlhammer, haven't you, Druce?'

The gargoyle nodded. 'Gargoyle friends,' he said. He licked the giant's bald head then grinned at Tiana.

Ulf hopped in the front beside Dr Fielding.

'Ready?' she asked.

'Ready,' Ulf replied.

Tiana perched on the dashboard. 'Me too.'

Dr Fielding started the engine and drove to the gates. 'Open,' she called.

The gates opened automatically, and they sped off up the driveway.

Ulf was still wondering about the Professor's message: *The Prisoner is More Dangerous than you think.* What did it mean?

Then he giggled as Druce's face appeared upside-down at the windscreen. 'Woohoo,' the gargoyle gurgled. '**Howwwwwlhammer, here we come!**'

CHAPTER FOUR

The RSPCB truck headed northwards all morning, trundling along leafy lanes. Ulf looked out of the window at the open countryside: green hills and valleys, hedgerows and patchwork fields. The further they travelled the more excited he became; Ulf loved going on expeditions and seeing beasts in the wild. Gradually, he noticed the landscape changing, becoming more rugged. They turned off the road and drove across a vast tract of moorland into remote wilderness, then ahead of them he saw a forest.

'That's Howling Forest,' Dr Fielding said. 'Howlhammer Castle's not far now.' She drove the truck in between the trees, bumping over logs and roots on to a muddy track.

Ulf looked up through the windscreen and saw the trees' branches were knotted and gnarled. He could hear the sound of the wind howling through them and, as the branches swayed, he glimpsed stormclouds overhead. Rain began falling on the windscreen.

'Where's the sun gone?' Tiana asked, pressing her hands against the glass.

Dr Fielding turned on the truck's wipers. 'Oh, everything's different at Howlhammer,' she said. 'Even the weather.'

Ulf sat up in his seat, intrigued, as they drove past mighty barbwood trees and along the banks of an overgrown stream. He saw a flock of black-bearded rooks take off from a thicket then a flash of white as something ran past through the forest. It was a unicorn! 'Tiana, look!' Ulf said. He saw another unicorn following the first. They both veered on to the muddy track, galloping ahead of the truck.

'They're beautiful!' Tiana exclaimed.

'A herd of unicorns live wild around Howlhammer,' Dr Fielding said. 'Those two are probably heading to the same place we are.' She drove on, following the unicorns through the forest and up a steep hill.

At the hill's summit, the trees thinned and Ulf saw an enormous stone wall ahead. He looked up, glimpsing dark jagged turrets. 'Howlhammer Castle!' he said excitedly.

Two huge wooden doors opened in the castle wall and the unicorns galloped inside. Dr Fielding drove after them into a large cobbled courtyard surrounded by high walls.

At one end of the courtyard Ulf saw the main castle building. It was made from solid stone, standing sheer like a cliff with towers rising from it and a flag at its top.

'It's huge,' he said.

'It was once a royal castle,' Dr Fielding explained.

Ulf glanced around trying to take it all in. He saw knights in armour leading the unicorns to a stable block. 'Ghost knights,' he whispered to Tiana.

Dr Fielding parked the truck in front of the main building, and Ulf looked up in awe. It looked even bigger up close. There were creeper vines hanging from its stone balconies, and it had dark slits for windows. He saw high walkways and stone gargoyles leering down.

Druce leapt from the truck's roof cackling at the top of his voice, 'Wakey-wakey, gargoyles! Drucey here!'

Ulf got out into the rain and saw the castle's gargoyles turn from stone to flesh as Druce clambered up to play with them.

He could hear moanings and groanings coming from the castle's windows, and a shiver ran up his spine. Ghosts, he thought.

Orson stepped from the truck and patted the castle's stone. 'This place is over six hundred years old, Ulf. Rock solid it is.'

'Right then,' Dr Fielding said. 'Shall we go inside and find out what's been happening here?'

'I'll be checking on the unicorns if you need me, Dr Fielding,' Orson said. He looked at Ulf. 'Good luck in there. Rather you than me.' And he strode off across the courtyard towards the stable block.

Ulf turned to Dr Fielding who was sheltering under a stone arch at the castle's doorway. 'Why isn't Orson coming with us?' he asked.

'He's not keen on the ghosts here, Ulf. Between you and me, he gets a bit spooked. I'll call him on the walkie-talkie if we need him.'

Tiana flew to her shoulder. 'Hold on a sec — if Orson's scared to go inside then I am too.'

'You'll be fine,' Dr Fielding reassured them both. 'You may find it a little strange at first because it's dark inside, but please try not to panic.' She handed Ulf a torch. 'Take this and keep close. Tiana, you can use your sparkles.'

Ulf wiped the rain from his face, then edged past Dr Fielding, pretending he wasn't afraid. 'I'll go first if you like,' he said.

'That's the spirit, Ulf. Spoken like a true RSPCB agent.'

Ulf reached for the large iron handle on the castle's door, but before he could even touch it, the door creaked open. He took a deep breath and stepped inside.

CHAPTER FIVE

At the top of a tall tree in Howling Forest, Baron Marackai was peering through his telescope. 'Splendid! My plan's working,' he muttered. He called down through the branches, 'The RSPCB have arrived.'

In a clearing below, Blud and Bone were packing away the hot-air balloon. They looked up. 'Is the w-w-werewolf with them, Sir?' Blud asked nervously.

'Yes,' the Baron said. 'Even that ugly gargoyle's here. We shall kill them all.' The Baron chuckled as he climbed down from the tree. 'Now, hurry up and pack the balloon with the rest of the stuff.'

'Yes, Sir,' Blud and Bone replied, ramming the balloon's silk into the basket. Parked in the woods was a tractor and trailer. Bone carried the balloon's basket and wedged it on to the trailer under a tarpaulin sheet.

Baron Marackai turned up the collar of his fur coat and glanced through the trees. 'Any luck yet, Harold?' he called.

On the edge of the clearing, the headless man was walking by a stream, turning the head in his hand this way and that, scanning the forest. He lifted it up to look back at the Baron. 'It'sss thissss way,' he hissed.

Blud tugged the Baron's coat. 'Harold gives me the creeps, Sir,' he said. 'It's not natural to talk with your head chopped off.'

Baron Marackai whispered, 'I wouldn't let him hear you speak like that.'

'Why, Sir?'

'Because it could upset him, and he might do this...' The Baron punched Blud on the nose.

'Ouch!'

'Now shut up and start the tractor!'

'Des, Dir. Right away, Dir.'

Blud and Bone climbed up into the tractor's cab, and the Baron stepped on to its footplate. 'Follow Harold!' he ordered.

The tractor began chugging through the forest behind the headless man.

'Where's he going, Sir?' Bone asked.

'He's looking for something,' the Baron replied. 'SOMETHING BEASTLY THAT WILL TEAR THE RSPCB TO PIECES.'

Blud and Bone glanced at one another excitedly.

'Is it a monster, Sir?' Blud asked.

'Oh, it's better than that,' the Baron said.

Blud and Bone glanced at one another again.

Bone put his hand up. 'Sir, is it two monsters?'

Blud put up his hand. 'Or a two-headed monster, Sir?'

'Shut up, you idiots,' the Baron snapped. 'I'm not telling you. It's my plan. Now drive!'

They drove on, following Headless Harold as he searched the forest.

'Sir, permission to speak, Sir,' Blud said. 'How did you know the RSPCB would come?'

The Baron chuckled. 'Because I'm a genius,' he replied. 'And they're in for quite a surprise.'

CHAPTER SIX

Ulf shone his torch into the gloom. He was in the castle's Great Hall, a large stone room with a vaulted ceiling and rusted shields on its walls.

Tiana sparkled softly beside him. 'It's cold,' she whispered.

'The castle's not been lived in for centuries,' Dr Fielding explained.

Ulf heard footsteps coming across the room towards them. He shone his torch but there was no one there.

'It's just a ghost, Ulf,' Dr Fielding said. 'They're all around us.'

Ulf crept forward nervously, the stone floor cold under his bare feet. He shone his torchbeam on to a long banqueting table and saw it was thick with dust. A wooden goblet floated up from it, then, at the other end of the table, he heard a scraping sound as a chair slid out by itself.

'Ulf, this is creepy,' Tiana said, clinging to his T-shirt.

Ulf shone his torch to his left, hearing moaning and groaning coming from a dark open fireplace. Then, suddenly, he heard a shield rattle on the wall and he swung his light towards it. The shield fell to the floor and a deep cackling laughter echoed around the hall.

'Don't be spooked, Ulf,' Dr Fielding said. 'It's just a fearfinder, a mischievous species of ghost.'

She walked to a stone archway at the side of the room and parted a sheet of cobwebs. 'Zazz, we're here,' she called.

'Zazz? Who's Zazz?' Ulf asked, stepping beside her.

'He's an RSPCB Keeper who looks after the ghosts here,' Dr Fielding explained. 'It will have been him who sent the message.'

'You mean someone stays here?'Tiana asked. 'They must be crazy.'

'Zazz is a genie, Tiana,' Dr Fielding replied. 'Genies can see ghosts, and are perfectly suited to haunted habitats.' She stepped through the archway shining her torch. 'Zazz, we're here.'

But there was no reply.

'Come on, you two. Let's find him and see what the trouble is.' Dr Fielding headed down a long dark corridor.

Ulf crept after her, hearing quiet voices all around him. The walls were whispering, cracks in the stone moving like mouths. He shone his torch left and right into dusty rooms. In one, an open book was floating, its pages turning by themselves. In the next, coins were moving across a table, stacking themselves into piles. In another, a wooden spoon was stirring in a pot. All the rooms were haunted.

Dr Fielding turned off the corridor into a dark chamber. Ulf shone his torch and the light glinted on piles of weapons: shields, swords, pikes and spears. The floor felt sticky underfoot – it was oozing with green ectoplasm!

They continued to another room and, as Ulf stepped in, his torchlight illuminated large tapestries on its walls. He could make out images of knights on unicorns riding into battle.

'Hey, look at this pretty chair,' Tiana said.

Ulf saw the fairy sparkling above a tall wooden chair at the side of the room. It was encrusted with jewels.

'That's the throne of King Stephen,' Dr Fielding told her. 'He lived here over five hundred years ago, and his ghost still haunts the castle.'

Ulf smiled. 'I wonder if he's sitting on it now, Tiana.'

Tiana shot away from the throne, and darted into Ulf's pocket. 'That wasn't funny, Ulf,' she said.

'Come on, keep up,' Dr Fielding told them, stepping out of the room into a narrow passageway. She called again, 'Zazz, we're here.'

As Ulf followed her, his hand brushed against the passageway's stone wall. The wall felt wet. He shone his torch and saw blood trickling from veins in the stone. The wall was bleeding! He heard squeaking and saw vampire rats licking the floor. He hurried as fast as he could to keep up with Dr Fielding.

At the passageway's end they came out into a wide hallway and Ulf heard the ding-ding of a bell. Suddenly, out of the darkness, a bicycle came rattling towards them, its pedals turning by themselves. Surprised, he jumped aside, letting it pass, then stared as it sped away round a corner.

Tiana peered from Ulf's pocket. 'Was that a ghost riding a bicycle?' she asked.

'That's one of the ghosts that Professor Farraway brought here,' Dr Fielding replied. 'The Professor relocated many new ghosts here from haunted habitats that were under threat.'

Ulf imagined Professor Farraway, over fifty years ago, walking through these very same corridors and rooms.

'Zazz, are you here?' Dr Fielding called again.

'I'm upstairs by the spying eyes,' a distant voice called back.

'At last,' Dr Fielding said. She turned up an enormous flight of stone steps, and Ulf and Tiana followed her, heading up and up through the castle. They stepped out on the top floor into a corridor that had dusty portraits on its walls. Ulf shone his torch at the portraits and saw the faces of lords and ladies staring back, their eyes moving to look at him.

'Zazz, where are you exactly?' Dr Fielding called.

'I'm right here,' a voice said. There was a bright flash then a puff of purple smoke. A chubby figure formed from the smoke, floating in mid-air. It had friendly blue eyes and a pointy beard, and its body swept down into a wispy purple tail. 'Dr Fielding, thank goodness you came,' the genie said.

'Hello, Zazz. I'd like you to meet Ulf and Tiana,' Dr Fielding replied.

The genie smiled. 'Super salutations to you both,' he said, his right arm growing and stretching down to Ulf, his left arm turning spaghetti-thin and holding out a tiny hand for Tiana.

Ulf and Tiana shook hands with the genie and both giggled. His hands felt tingly.

'We got your message, Zazz,' Dr Fielding said. 'You said there'd been some kind of trouble?'

'Something rather baffling,' Zazz replied. 'Follow me and I'll show you.'

The genie floated down the Corridor of Spying Eyes, and stopped by a door at its end. 'I've gathered them all in here,' he said.

'Gathered what?' Dr Fielding asked.

Ulf could hear voices coming from behind the door.

'Brace yourselves for a surprise,' Zazz said. The genie turned to smoke and slid under the door, then a second later opened it from the other side. 'Behold!'

Ulf saw a bright candlelit room crowded with people drinking and dancing.

Tiana smiled. 'It's a party!'

'So you can see them too?' Zazz said. 'Then it's as I thought.' The genie looked at Dr Fielding, concerned. 'I don't know how this could have happened. They've got bodies now. They're flesh and blood.'

'This is trouble indeed,' Dr Fielding said, stepping into the room.

'I don't understand,' Ulf said. 'Who are these people?' They looked very strange. Ulf saw one with a huge hole in his stomach and another with her hair standing on end.

Zazz floated beside Ulf. **'They're not normal people, Ulf. They're ghosts. They've come to life!'**

CHAPTER SEVEN

With the genie floating at his side, Ulf entered the room. 'How can ghosts come back to life, Zazz?' he whispered.

The genie shrugged his purple shoulders. 'I've never known anything like it.'

Ulf walked through the crowd, glancing left and right at the strangest mix of characters he'd ever seen: a man with an arrow in his eye... a maid with boils on her face... a court jester with a twisted neck... a woman draped in seaweed... a bone-thin monk...

Then a grey-faced man smiled at Ulf and held up a glass of wine. 'To a happy day!' the man said. 'I see you've got your body back too.'

As the man sipped from his glass, Ulf noticed his lips were pale blue, and split and cracked. Ulf backed away nervously.

'That's Poisoned Pete,' Zazz whispered. 'He's supposed to be a poltergeist.'

'But he's got a body.'

'Normally he hasn't. Normally he haunts the royal wine store invisibly, knocking over the bottles.'

Ulf accidentally stepped on a woman's foot. 'Sorry,' he said to her.

The woman was white with frost. 'N–n–no harm d–done,' she replied. She slipped her shoe off and Ulf saw her toes were solid icicles.

'P–p–pleased to m–meet you,' she said, her teeth chattering. 'L–lovely to b–be alive a–g–gain, isn't it–t?'

Ulf smiled at her nervously.

'That's Frozen Nell,' Zazz whispered. 'She's normally a sprite and drifts up the stairwell like an icy draft.'

'Ahoy there!' a man in a sailor's uniform called to Ulf. The man started laughing.

'And that's the Hollow Admiral. He's normally a ghoul, and haunts the battlements laughing.'

The Hollow Admiral stepped over and Ulf saw he had a large hole in his middle. The admiral poked his hand through it, wiggled his fingers and laughed again. 'Ha ha ha! Got in the way of a cannonball!' he said.

Ulf could see clear through him.

'Mind out, Ulf!' a tiny voice called. Tiana came zooming through the Hollow Admiral, then darted up and hid behind the brim of his hat.

'Tiana, what are you doing?' Ulf asked.

The fairy peeped down. 'Shhhh, I'm playing hide and seek, Ulf. Pretend you haven't seen me.'

'Coming, ready or not!' Ulf heard. He saw a boy rush over with fungus growing from his skin. The boy looked behind Ulf then under the Admiral's legs. 'Where is that fairy?' he muttered, then he hurried on through the crowd.

'That one's Henry the Hidden,' Zazz whispered to Ulf. 'He's a Lost Soul – he died when he hid up a tree and wasn't found until it was too late.'

Ulf gulped. He was finding this all so strange. Everyone in the room had once been dead.

Zazz led him through the crowd pointing out who each one was: the man with the arrow through his eye was Tom the Target, and the woman with her hair standing on end was Lightning Lil. Then there was the Drowned Duchess... the Hungry Monk... the Clumsy Jester... the Bubonic Maid... and a man with a guitar smashed over his head called Highly-strung Sam. All of them should have been ghosts, but they were now very much alive again.

Ulf felt something poke his back. 'Hands up!' he heard. He span round and saw a caped man in a bloodstained shirt pointing a pistol at him. Ulf put his hands in the air.

'Only joking,' the man said. He slid the pistol into his belt, grabbed Ulf's hand and gave it a vigorous shake. 'Duelling Duke's the name. Pleased to meet you.'

'He's normally a phantom,' Zazz whispered to Ulf.

Ulf noticed the Duke's hand glistening as he shook it.

'Now, where's that pretty little maid?' the Duke said, letting go. 'I fancy a kiss.' He swished his cape then strode off.

Zazz zipped after him. 'Duke, please leave the Bubonic Maid alone,' the genie called. 'She's got the plague, remember.'

Ulf noticed his own hand glistening now too. He looked at it closely and saw golden droplets on his fingers.

Tiana came whizzing over from the Hollow Admiral's hat. 'Hey, pretty glitter,' she said, perching on Ulf's middle finger. As she bent to look at a golden droplet, her dress of dried cornflowers brushed against it. Instantly, the dried cornflowers started blooming, their colour changing from pale to bright blue. 'Wow, look at me!' the fairy said, twirling in the air.

Ulf stared in amazement. **The golden droplet had brought the flowers on Tiana's dress back to life!**

Ulf looked around the room at the ghosts. I wonder… he thought, and he ran to find Dr Fielding. She was at the side of the room examining the Hungry Monk. 'Dr Fielding,' he said, holding out his hand to show her the golden droplets. 'Have you seen this stuff? It was on the Duelling Duke. It brought Tiana's cornflowers to life.' He pointed to the fairy flying across the room in her dress of blue blooming cornflowers.

'My goodness,' Dr Fielding said, seeing her.

'Dr Fielding, if these golden droplets can bring flowers to life, do you think they could bring ghosts to life too?' he asked.

'I'm not really—'

'Look, there's more here,' Ulf said, seeing golden droplets on the foot of the Hungry Monk.

Dr Fielding looked down at the monk's foot. It was sparkling. 'You might be on to something, Ulf,' she replied.

She stepped away and walked among the crowd. Ulf followed and together they checked each ghost closely. Every one had golden droplets on them.

Dr Fielding gestured to Zazz to come over. In a flash and a puff of smoke, the genie appeared at her side.

'Zazz, have you checked the Potions Room lately?' she asked. 'A poltergeist couldn't have got in there and knocked a potion over, could it?'

Zazz's eyes glanced to Poisoned Pete. 'Quite possibly, Dr Fielding. Why do you ask?'

'These ghosts are all contaminated with a golden chemical. I think it may be a potion that's brought them to life.'

'A potion? How incredible!' Zazz said. 'I'll go and see if anything's been spilled.'

'Can I go too, Dr Fielding?' Ulf asked. He liked the sound of a Potions Room.

'Of course you can,' Dr Fielding replied. 'In the meantime, I'll gather some samples.' She turned to the genie. 'Zazz, could you keep all the other ghosts off this floor of the castle to avoid any risk of contamination. This is a quarantine room now.'

Zazz bowed. 'As you wish,' he said. Then he glanced at Ulf. 'Let's go.'

Ulf suddenly felt himself rising off the ground. 'Hey, what's happening?' he asked.

Zazz smiled. 'Don't worry, it's genie power,' he said.

Ulf was floating in the air. 'You mean *you're* doing this?'

'That's right,' Zazz replied. **'Let's travel genie-style!'**

CHAPTER EIGHT

Ulf glided alongside the genie, drifting through the castle's corridors, his feet high off the ground. It felt fantastic, as if the air was carrying him. He ran his hand along the cold stone ceiling, shining his torch at bats hanging upside-down asleep. He ducked under archways and tilted his body to turn corners. He pushed through cobwebs and saw giant spiders scurry away. He saw bugbeasts peering from cracks in the walls and longhorn beetles crawling on the floor below. 'Zazz, this is brilliant!' he said.

'It's the best way to travel,' the genie replied. 'Much quicker than walking.' He led Ulf to the castle's upper-east wing, then down a narrow passage. Ulf felt himself slowly descend and his feet gently touched down in front of a small black door.

'Here we are: the Potions Room,' Zazz said. He whirled like smoke and threaded himself through the door's keyhole. A moment later, the door creaked open and Zazz peered round it from the other side. He gestured for Ulf to enter.

As Ulf stepped into the room, the acrid smell of chemicals filled his nose. He shone his torch and its beam illuminated bottles of coloured liquids. There were row upon row of them, lining the walls. He could see every colour imaginable: ice blue... poppy red... bright yellow... emerald green... glowing mauve...

Zazz hovered above a large cauldron in the centre of the room, his eyes gleaming. 'Pretty in here, isn't it?' he said.

'Are these all potions?' Ulf asked, shining his torch along the bottles.

'They're the royal medicines from hundreds

of years ago. In olden times, humans tried to treat everything with potions. Some of them are quite peculiar.'

Ulf stepped to the wall and blew dust from a bottle full of orange syrup. It had a label on it: **Tropical Lava for Happiness,** he read. He blew the dust from another containing green sludge: **Swamp Slime for Acne.** He saw **Snoozejuice for Insomnia... Thunderbolt Brew for Energy... Cuckoo Spit for Burns... Fungus Fudge for Constipation... Clever Brandy for Brains... Toad Wax for Dry Skin...**

'Everything seems to be in order,' Zazz said. 'I can't see any sign of a disturbance.'

'We'd better be sure,' Ulf said. He shone his torch around, looking to see if a golden potion had spilled anywhere. He checked the floor, then up and down the shelves, but there were no bottles tipped over or smashed. As he continued checking, a shining silver potion caught his eye: **Moonjuice for Werewolves.**

Ulf picked it up excitedly. He'd encountered moonjuice before. It was the silver nectar of a night-flowering plant that stored the moon's energy, and could trigger a werewolf transformation. 'What's moonjuice doing here, Zazz?' he asked.

But there was no reply. Ulf looked round and saw that the genie had vanished. 'Zazz?'

From the corridor, he heard Zazz's voice calling, 'Your Majesty, this area is out of bounds today. Please go downstairs!' Then came deep moans and groans.

Ulf quickly placed the moonjuice back on the shelf and poked his head out of the door to see what was happening. He shone his torch down the corridor and saw Zazz chasing after a floating sword and crown, calling frantically, 'Not that way, Your Majesty!'

Your Majesty? Ulf thought. He remembered the throne he'd seen downstairs. It must be the ghost of King Stephen! Ulf watched as Zazz pursued the crown and sword up a flight of steps. He heard a door opening and the sound of wind and rain.

'Your Majesty, no!' he heard Zazz shout.

Ulf crept after them. He climbed the steps to an open arched door that led outside into the wind and rain. Ahead of him was a walkway leading to the top of a tall tower. He could see Zazz by a barred door at the walkway's end. The King's sword was swishing back and forth against the bars, while the genie tried to grab hold of its handle.

'Your Majesty, stop that!' Zazz shouted.

'Are you okay, Zazz?' Ulf called.

The genie snatched the sword, then came zipping back over the walkway towards Ulf. 'Mind out. I'm coming through!'

Ulf turned sideways as Zazz flew inside, the sword missing Ulf's nose by millimetres. Then he saw the crown coming too, following the genie. The crown flew over Ulf's head and he felt goosebumps prickle all over his body as the ghost of the King passed straight through him.

Ulf shivered and gripped the archway to steady himself. He was about to head back inside when he noticed something golden glistening on the barred door of the tower. He stepped along the walkway to take a closer look. On the bars and on its padlock were golden droplets. The padlock looked broken. Ulf slid the bolt and pushed the door open, stepping into a cold, round chamber that had rusted chains hanging on its walls. He saw more golden droplets on the chamber's floor.

There was a flash, then a puff of smoke, and Zazz appeared in the doorway. 'Sorry about that, Ulf. King Stephen was on his haunting rounds. He's in a strange mood toda—' Zazz stopped talking and looked again at the open door. 'How did you get in here?'

'The padlock was broken, Zazz,' Ulf explained. 'Look, there are golden droplets here.'

'Gadzooks!' the genie exclaimed, his blue eyes widening. His neck stretched and he looked around the chamber: first to the chains on the wall, then to the golden droplets on the floor. 'He's escaped!' the genie cried.

'Escaped? Who's escaped, Zazz?'

'Headless Harold, the ghost who haunts this

tower.' Zazz's head started spinning.

'Zazz, are you okay?' Ulf asked.

'Not really,' the genie replied. 'Harold's a spectre, Ulf, and you know what they're like.'

Ulf shook his head.

'They're no good,' the genie whispered. 'Harold's the ghost of a prisoner.' Zazz glanced nervously to his left, then to his right. 'This is the castle's prison tower, Ulf. Every day the King's ghost comes to check that Harold's still locked up. Oh, no wonder the King's agitated today!' Zazz looked at the droplets on the floor, and turned cross-eyed with worry. 'Harold must have come to life too. **Gadzooks, a living spectre! It doesn't bear thinking about!** I'd better go and find him. You can make your own way back, can't you, Ulf?'

'Er, I think—'

'Super,' Zazz interrupted and, with a flash and a puff of smoke, the genie vanished.

Ulf was left alone in the cold prison tower. He glanced at the chains on the wall. An escaped prisoner, he thought. He remembered the warning that Professor Farraway's ghost had written in the dust earlier that day: *The Prisoner is More Dangerous Than You Think.*

Ulf felt himself getting the heebie-jeebies. The wind was whistling through the bars of the door. Feeling anxious, he hurried off to tell Dr Fielding.

★　★　★

Deep in Howling Forest, Baron Marackai, Blud and Bone were chugging through the trees on the tractor, following Headless Harold.

'Is it a ten-headed monster, Sir?' Blud asked.

'Shut up, I'm not telling.'

'Is it a hundred-headed monster, Sir?' Bone asked.

'Oh, will you nincompoops be quiet!'

'Go on, Sir, tell us what it is.'

'SILENCE! You'll have to wait and see...'

CHAPTER NINE

As Ulf approached the door of the Quarantine Room, he heard singing: 'Put your left leg in, your left leg out. In, out, in, out. Shake it all about!'

'Tiana's got them playing party games,' Dr Fielding called from the room opposite. She was holding up a test tube of golden droplets, inspecting them by the light of a small window. 'I've managed to take a sample. Did you have any luck in the Potions Room?' she asked.

Ulf stepped inside to tell her what had happened. 'No, we were interrupted by the ghost of King Stephen. It turns out that the ghost of a prisoner has escaped – a spectre.'

'Escaped?' she asked.

'Yes, there were golden droplets in the prison tower too. The ghost must have come back to life. Zazz has gone searching for it.'

Dr Fielding looked back at the test tube then frowned. 'This is all getting rather out of hand, isn't it?'

'Are spectres dangerous, Dr Fielding?' Ulf asked.

'Spectres are vengeful ghosts, Ulf. They can cause all sorts of trouble. I hope Zazz finds it soon.'

Suddenly, a ghostly figure appeared at the window behind her. Ulf jumped back, startled.

'Wooohooo! Wooohoooo!' the ghostly figure gurgled.

Dr Fielding smiled at it. 'Hmm, a bedsheet ghost. I've never seen one of those before.'

The ghostly figure hopped up and down then blew a raspberry. 'Blurgh! Fooled you!'

It was Druce wearing a bedsheet. The gargoyle poked his ugly face out and Ulf saw him giggling.

'Druce, are you trying to scare us?' Ulf asked.

'Drucey gaaarghost,' the gargoyle gurgled. Then he scampered away up the castle wall calling, 'Woohoo woohoo!'

Dr Fielding stepped to a table and placed the test tube of golden liquid into a wooden rack. 'So there wasn't a spillage in the Potions Room. Hmm, that is puzzling,' she said. Beside the test-tube rack was a portable microscope. She sat down in front of it. 'I can't think where else this liquid could have come from.' Dr Fielding dripped a few drops of the golden liquid on to a glass slide and placed it under the microscope.

'What potion is it?' Ulf asked.

Dr Fielding adjusted the focus on the microscope. 'I've got a hunch what it might be but I need to examine it more closely.'

'There were all kinds of potions in that room, Dr Fielding. There was even moonjuice.'

Dr Fielding looked up. 'I hope you left it where it was, Ulf. You're training to be an agent, remember. No transforming while you're here.'

'How come there's moonjuice here?' Ulf asked. 'Did werewolves once live in the castle?'

Dr Fielding chuckled. 'No, Ulf. Once upon a time, humans used to drink moonjuice as a cure for baldness, to make their hair grow. It didn't turn them into wolves, though.'

For baldness? Ulf thought. He cast his mind back to the bottle of silver liquid in the Potions Room. He felt sure it had said, **for Werewolves**.

'Could you do me a favour please, Ulf, and fetch Tiana from the Quarantine Room? I'd like the ghosts to settle down now.'

'No problem, Dr Fielding,' Ulf replied, walking to the door. 'Then I'll look for the ghost that's escaped.'

'No, Ulf, let Zazz deal with that. And don't worry. It'll turn up sooner or later… **spectres have a way of appearing when you're least expecting them.**'

CHAPTER TEN

Back in Howling Forest, Headless Harold stopped walking. He held his head aloft in the rain, turning it to look back. 'Thissss issss the place,' he hissed.

Baron Marackai jumped down from the tractor, his serpent-skin boots sinking into thick red mud. He squelched over to the headless man. 'It's here?' he asked. 'Definitely?'

Harold's eyes looked down. 'Right under our feeeeet.'

The Baron smiled. 'That's splendid news,' he said. 'Now the RSPCB are doomed!' He called over to Blud and Bone, 'Park up and unload the equipment!'

The Baron and Harold sheltered under a tree as Blud and Bone climbed down from the tractor and untied the trailer's tarpaulin. Blud unloaded baseball bats, ropes and chains, piling them on the ground. Bone lifted down motorbikes and wheeled them into lines.

'What's all this stuff for, Sir?' Bone called.

'Wait and see,' the Baron replied.

Blud and Bone whispered to one another, then Blud came squelching through the mud and tugged on the hem of the Baron's coat. 'Sir, this thing that's going to tear the RSPCB to pieces, is it a—'

'Oh, for pity's sake!' the Baron snapped. He grabbed Blud by the collar and pushed the small man's face into the muddy ground. 'It's right underneath us.'

'Is it a *mud* monster, Sir?' Blud mumbled, his mouth full of mud.

'No, you nitwit! It's much better than that.' The Baron kicked Blud away, then turned to Harold. 'Now, Harold, I need another small favour from you. It concerns a mountain giant.'

He took Harold's head from under his arm and whispered in its ear.

'Yessss,' the head said.

The Baron whispered some more.

'Oooooo,' the head said.

And more.

'Now that'sssssss *eeeeevil*,' the head said.

'So, what do you think, then?'

'Let'ssss do it.' Harold's head grinned then looked at its body. 'Go!' it said, and the headless body went running off through the trees.

Baron Marackai smiled. 'Thank you, Harold, my evil friend. NOTHING CAN STOP US NOW.'

CHAPTER ELEVEN

As Ulf and Tiana went downstairs to the courtyard, Ulf told the fairy about the missing ghost. He stepped outside and looked up through the rain at the prison tower high on the castle – it stood alone against the grey sky. 'That's where the prisoner should be, Tiana,' he said, pointing towards it. 'The Professor warned us about a prisoner, remember.'

Tiana circled Ulf's head, giggling. 'Ulf, it's not a *real* prisoner. It's just a ghost,' she said. 'Come on, let's go to the stable block to see Orson and the unicorns; my wings are getting soaked out here.' And she zoomed away across the courtyard.

Ulf hesitated. Looking up at the prison tower, he felt a creepy sensation that he couldn't quite explain.

'Keep up, Ulf!'

The rain was lashing Ulf's face. He looked away and hurried after the fairy, heading towards the shelter of the stable block.

The stable was a large covered area at the side of the courtyard. It was bustling with activity, crowded with ghost knights and unicorns. Ulf saw Orson kneeling by a unicorn mare, inspecting its teeth.

Tiana called to the giant, 'Hi, Orson. What are you doing?'

'Hello, you two,' Orson said, as Ulf and Tiana came over. 'The rain's bringing the unicorns in so I'm helping the ghost knights to give them a check-up. Dry yourselves off and you can help too.'

Tiana shook the raindrops from her wings, and Ulf picked up a clump of clean straw from the stable floor and rubbed it over his wet hair. He glanced around, intrigued by what the ghost knights were doing. Some were loading hay into feeding bays, one was shovelling manure into a wheelbarrow, and another was scrubbing a unicorn's hooves. 'I didn't realise that the ghost knights took care of the unicorns,' he said to Orson.

'Oh, yes,' the giant replied. 'These knights have looked after the unicorns of Howlhammer for centuries.'

Orson stood up and gave the unicorn mare a stroke. 'This one's in good health,' he called to a ghost knight. The giant washed his big hands in a barrel of water, and the ghost knight led the unicorn away. 'So, how are you two, then? Did you sort out the trouble in the castle?'

'Some of the ghosts have come back to life,' Tiana said.

Orson raised his eyebrows. 'Blimey, that's unusual!'

'And a ghost prisoner has escaped,' Ulf added.

Orson frowned. 'Escaped, eh?' He gestured for Ulf to step back as a knight in armour led another unicorn over beside them. 'Do you two want to give me a hand with this one?' he asked.

The unicorn was a stallion, twice Ulf's height, with a horn over two metres long. It was wet and muddy.

'Now, be careful,' Orson said. 'Unicorns may look pretty but they're powerful beasts and they've got a mean kick on them. First thing is to get it settled.' Orson took a handful of acorns from his pocket. 'Feed it these, Ulf. They should do the trick.'

Ulf took the acorns and held them up to the beast.

'Keep your hand flat so it doesn't nibble your fingers.'

Ulf felt the unicorn's lips close around the acorns and its rough tongue slide across his palm.

'That's it. Now he's happy.'

Ulf saw the ghost knight kneel down and begin scrubbing the unicorn's muddy hooves with a stiff brush.

'You can groom its coat and tail if you like, Ulf,' Orson said. 'I'll check its teeth.'

Ulf took a brush from a hook on a beam and set to work grooming the coarse white hair on the unicorn's flanks. The unicorn's body felt muscular and its wet hide smelt musky.

'Nice strong strokes, Ulf,' the giant said.

'What about me, Orson? What can I do?' Tiana asked.

'There's another over there I think you'll like, Tiana,' Orson replied, pointing towards a female unicorn lying asleep in the straw. Nestled beside her was a newborn foal.

'Oh, wow, a baby unicorn!' Tiana said.

'She's only a couple of days old,' Orson said. The foal had a small bump on its forehead where its horn would one day grow. 'Do you want to keep an eye on her while her mother gets some rest?'

'Yes, please!' Tiana said. She flew off and Ulf saw her perch in the straw beside the baby unicorn. 'It's got funny little whiskers,' she called, tickling the foal under its chin.

Ulf liked helping Orson. It reminded him of being back in the beast park at Farraway Hall.

As he brushed the stallion, he watched the giant lift the beast's upper lip and rub his finger along its gums. 'They sometimes get abscesses from eating razorthorn bushes,' Orson explained. He tapped the unicorn's teeth with his fingernail. 'Good set of gnashers on this one, though.'

Ulf heard squeaking and looked down. The sound was coming from the ghost knight's armour as he scrubbed the unicorn's hooves.

'The rain rusts them, Ulf,' Orson said. From his pocket the giant took a tub of grease and wiped a dollop on to the knight's shoulder to ease the armour joint. The squeaking stopped and Orson winked at Ulf. 'No one likes to be a squeaker.'

Ulf ducked under the unicorn and brushed its other side. After that, he began brushing the unicorn's long white tail. Its hair was tangled and had twigs in it.

'That's it. Get all the bits out, Ulf,' Orson said.

As Ulf swept the brush down the tail's length, the unicorn flicked it gently from side to side. Then, when the tail was clean, Ulf walked to the front of the beast and reached up to brush its long white mane.

Ulf saw Orson scoop brown wax from the unicorn's ear with his finger.

'Their ears are always getting clogged,' the giant said. Orson wiped his finger in the straw to clean it.

'I've finished, Orson. It's all brushed,' Ulf told him.

The giant inspected Ulf's work. 'Beautiful,' he said. 'Its coat's nice and shiny now. Just one last thing to do.'

The giant took a big handkerchief from his shirt pocket. He ran the handkerchief up and down the unicorn's horn, giving it a polish. Ulf saw the horn shine – it was pearly white with spiral ridges running up its length.

'Imagine that charging at you in battle,' Orson said. 'It'd go straight through you.'

'In battle?' Ulf asked. 'What do you mean?'

'Unicorns are warrior beasts, Ulf. Hundreds of years ago they were the royal steeds. The King and his knights rode them into battle.'

The ghost knight stood up with a clank.

'All done?' Orson asked.

The ghost knight saluted.

'Take him away, then.'

Ulf stepped back as the knight led the unicorn to the back of the stables.

'These knights were once the bravest soldiers in the land, Ulf,' Orson explained. 'It was their job to protect the King.' The giant looked out from the stables at the castle's huge outer walls. 'Back then, this whole place was a fortress. Those walls were for keeping the King's enemies out. I wouldn't like to have lived here back then. Dangerous times they were.'

Ulf looked back up at the main castle building, to the prison tower at its top...

The Prisoner is More Dangerous Than You Think.

'Orson, do you know if ghosts can be dangerous?'

'Ghosts?' The giant scratched his bald head.

'Well, poltergeists can throw things at you, and phantoms can give you goosebumps—'

'What about spectres?'

'I'm no expert, Ulf, but I'd say that spectres are best left alone. One of them once caught me in the dark and it scared me silly.'

'What happened?' Ulf asked.

'I got the collywobbles, I did. Ran as fast as I could.'

Ulf wanted to know more about spectres. He handed Orson the brush. 'Thanks for letting me help,' he said, and he ran out into the rain.

'Are you off, Ulf?' Orson called.

'I just want to check something,' Ulf replied, and he ran across the courtyard to the RSPCB truck. He hopped into the front seat and, from his bag on the floor, took out *The Book of Beasts*. He turned its pages, flicking through Professor Farraway's notes, looking for an entry on ghosts. He flicked past tips on how to track a yeti, instructions for getting free from a spidron's web, and methods for growing carnivorous fungus. He stopped at an entry headed: GETTING TO KNOW GHOSTS.

Ghosts are non-corporeal beasts (beasts without bodies) made of leftover emotions from unresolved lives. They display repetitive habits from their pasts such as walking the same corridor to find something lost long ago. There is really no need to be frightened of most ghosts, since they usually have good intentions like righting a wrong. There is only one species I would say has bad intentions: spectres - ghosts born from bad lives. Be wary of these, and, if approaching one, always follow the first rule of non-corporeal cryptozoology: to know a ghost's intentions, you must first know its past.

Ulf closed the book and looked up through the truck's windscreen at the prison tower. Had the Professor really been warning him about the spectre in the tower?

Ulf's thoughts were interrupted by the sound of the castle gates opening. In the truck's rear view mirror he saw a man come staggering in to the courtyard. Ulf rubbed his eyes, surprised. The man had no head!

CHAPTER TWELVE

Ulf jumped from the truck as the headless man came into the courtyard. He saw ghost knights hurrying down the steps from the battlements on the outer wall, and more clanking from the stables, marching towards the man, unsheathing their swords.

As Ulf ran to see what was going on, Zazz came zipping from the castle.

'Knights, leave him! I'll deal with this,' the genie called. Zazz flew to the headless man. 'Harold, I've been looking for you everywhere! Come with me at once.'

It's Headless Harold, Ulf thought. The ghost prisoner.

Ulf saw Zazz float above Headless Harold and raise him into the air by genie power. They began flying across the courtyard towards the castle building.

Ulf raced after them. 'Zazz, where are you taking him?' he called.

'Up to the Quarantine Room,' Zazz replied. 'Open the door for me, will you?'

Ulf opened the door to the castle and followed Zazz and Headless Harold into the Great Hall. Ulf switched on his torch and shone it at Harold. Where his head should have been was the stump of his neck, and there were bloodstains around his collar. 'Zazz, how come his head was chopped off?' Ulf asked.

Zazz stopped in mid-air and glanced under the ghost's arm. 'Gadzooks! His head! He usually carries it under his arm! Oh crumbs, he must have dropped it on the way in. Ulf, will you get him upstairs while I go and find it?'

'Erm...' Ulf hesitated, worried by the thought of being left alone with a spectre. 'Zazz, I'm not—'

'Super,' Zazz interrupted and, with a flash and a puff of smoke, the genie vanished.

Ulf stood alone with Headless Harold. He heard hissing coming from the spectre's windpipe.

Ulf gulped, then pulled himself together – an RSPCB agent wouldn't be afraid, he thought. 'Follow me, Harold,' he said. Tentatively, he took hold of the spectre's arm and led him out of the Great Hall into the Whispering Corridor. Ulf led Headless Harold through the Weapons Room, then, as they passed through the Throne Room, he heard loud moaning and groaning. He saw King Stephen's crown and sword floating by the throne.

Suddenly, Ulf felt Harold tugging hard on his arm, pulling him quickly into the Bleeding Passage.

'Hey, slow down,' Ulf said.

But Harold started running, pulling Ulf down the length of the passage. Ulf glanced back, hearing a clattering sound, and shone his torch. The King's sword and crown were pursuing them. The spectre was trying to get away from the King!

Harold pulled Ulf across the hallway.

'This way, Harold,' Ulf said, directing him up the stone staircase. Ulf turned and called down, 'Stay back, Your Majesty. I'm taking Harold to the Quarantine Room.'

But the crown and the sword kept following.

Ulf and Harold ran as fast as they could up to the Corridor of Spying Eyes. But as they were rushing to the Quarantine Room door, Ulf felt an icy chill creep into him. Goosebumps began prickling his skin. Something strange was happening to him. The hilt of a sword suddenly pressed into his hand and a crown came to rest on his head.

Ulf felt his arm move by itself, pointing the sword at Harold's back. Harold raised his hands in surrender. Then, from Ulf's mouth, came a deep voice that wasn't his own, 'No more escaping for you, Harold. Get back to the prison tower!'

The King's ghost had entered Ulf's body and taken it over!

Ulf found himself marching Headless Harold down the corridor, pointing the sword at the spectre's back.

He blinked as torchlight shone in his eyes. It was Dr Fielding. 'Don't panic, Ulf! I'm on my way,' she called. She came running towards him carrying a metal canister. 'You've been possessed, Ulf,' she said. She pointed the canister at Ulf and twisted a nozzle on its front. There was a whooshing sound and Ulf felt the chill being sucked from him and the crown falling from his head. His hand let go of the sword and he felt his goosebumps receding. Dr Fielding was sucking up the King's ghost, drawing it into the canister. Ulf felt a sudden looseness in his muscles as the sword and crown clattered to the floor by his feet. He staggered, dizzy.

'Are you okay, Ulf?' Dr Fielding asked.

He could feel his body again. He shook out his arms. 'I… I think so,' he said. Then he looked at the metal canister. 'What is that thing?'

'It's a ghost canister, Ulf,' Dr Fielding said, tightening its nozzle. 'Used for transporting ghosts from one haunted habitat to another. The King's ghost will be fine in here until it calms down.'

Dr Fielding shone her torch at Headless Harold, and Ulf saw the spectre's shoulders shaking as if he was laughing.

'So this is the spectre that escaped, I assume,' Dr Fielding said. 'Hmm, a headless one. Where did you find him?'

'He was outside the castle,' Ulf told her. 'He came in a few minutes ago.'

Dr Fielding shone her torch on Harold's boots. They were covered in red mud and there were muddy bootprints all along the corridor. 'What on earth was he doing outside the castle?' she asked.

Ulf shrugged. 'I've no idea. I was trying to get him upstairs while Zazz went to look for his head.'

'Here, let me help you get him in with the others,' Dr Fielding said. She took hold of

Headless Harold's arm and, together with Ulf, walked the spectre back down the corridor. 'We'll have to keep an eye on this one, Ulf.'

CHAPTER THIRTEEN

In the Quarantine Room, the party had quietened down and the ghosts were relaxing. The Hollow Admiral, Tom the Target, the Hungry Monk and Highly-strung Sam were playing cards at a table. Henry the Hidden was hiding beneath it. The Duelling Duke and the Bubonic Maid were having a kiss and a cuddle, and Poisoned Pete was fixing himself an evening drink.

Ulf and Dr Fielding lowered Headless Harold's body into a comfortable armchair.

'He should be okay here,' Dr Fielding said. She glanced at Harold's muddy boots. 'Ulf, do you think you could clean him up for me while I get back to my work? I was just running some tests.'

'If you think it's safe,' Ulf said.

Dr Fielding handed Ulf a pack of tissues from her pocket. 'I'll only be across the corridor. Call me if you need anything.'

As Dr Fielding left the room, Ulf noticed the other ghosts staring at Harold, whispering to each other. The spectre sat upright, tapping his fingers on the arms of the chair.

'Right, Harold, let's get you cleaned up,' Ulf said. He rolled up Harold's muddy trouser legs and cringed – Harold's legs were grey and mottled. Ulf took a tissue from the packet and began wiping the mud from the spectre's boots.

Just then, Ulf felt a tap on his shoulder and turned round. He saw Poisoned Pete leaning down to whisper to him.

'Excuse me, Ulf, but who invited *him* to the party?' Poisoned Pete asked. 'He's not staying, is he?'

'For now he is,' Ulf said.

Poisoned Pete looked back at the other ghosts. 'He *is* staying,' he said.

The ghosts marched over together.

'But he can't stay in here. He's not welcome,' Tom the Target whispered to Ulf.

'He's a mean one,' the Hungry Monk said.

'He's a sp–sp–spectre,' Frozen Nell said.

'Come away from him, Ulf,' Poisoned Pete whispered, pulling Ulf back. 'He's no good.'

Ulf stepped back a pace from Headless Harold. 'How come none of you like him?' he asked.

The ghosts huddled round Ulf. 'Because he's baaad,' they whispered. 'He's the ghost of a bad man.'

Poisoned Pete took a sip of wine. 'I heard he was a highwayman who robbed the King's jewels.'

Ulf saw Headless Harold rub his hands together then crack his knuckles.

The Duelling Duke spun his pistol. 'I heard he was a kidnapper who stole the King's daughter.'

Ulf could hear Harold's windpipe wheezing with laughter.

Frozen Nell shivered. 'I heard he was a m-m-murderer who k-killed the K-King's brother.'

Ulf felt nervous. 'Are you all trying to spook me?' he asked.

'No, no, nooooo,' the ghosts murmured.

Then the Hollow Admiral laughed. 'Ha ha ha! I heard worse, Ulf. I heard he was the most evil man in the land, and it was the King who chopped off his head.'

The ghosts whispered to each other, exchanging views on how bad they thought Headless Harold was. Ulf wasn't sure what to think. They were all saying different things, but none of it sounded good.

'Well, at least he's not brought his head with him,' Lightning Lil said to the others. She turned to Ulf, 'All his head does is moan and groan. "Revenge this... revenge that... revenge, revenge, revenge..." If you ask me, he should be locked back up in the prison tower.'

At that moment, Henry the Hidden popped

up from behind Harold's armchair and tapped Harold on the shoulder. 'Found you! Ha ha!'

Harold's arm shot up, whacking Henry the Hidden on the chin.

'Ouch!' Henry cried.

Ulf rushed forwards, pulling Henry away. 'Hey, Harold, there's no need for that,' he said.

'You bully!' the Duelling Duke said, pointing his pistol at Harold.

'You're not welcome here,' the Bubonic Maid said.

'Yeah, get back to the tower, Harold,' the Hungry Monk added.

Ulf turned to the crowd. 'Step away, everyone, please. Dr Fielding says he has to stay in here.'

The ghosts murmured their disapproval, but Ulf ushered them across the room. As he did, Dr Fielding popped her head around the door. 'Is everything all right in here, Ulf?' she asked.

'It's Headless Harold. The other ghosts don't like him,' Ulf told her.

The ghosts huddled at the far end of the

room, keeping their distance from the spectre. Harold was shaking his fist at them.

'Well, they'll all just have to get along for now,' Dr Fielding said. 'We can't let any of them out while they're contaminated.' She beckoned Ulf over excitedly. 'Ulf, come with me a moment,' she said. 'I've had a breakthrough. I know what that potion is – I know why the ghosts have come to life.'

CHAPTER FOURTEEN

Ulf and Dr Fielding went into her workroom. 'Have a look through the microscope,' Dr Fielding said.

Ulf stepped to the table and looked down the microscope's eyepiece. He could see floating golden hexagonal shapes.

'That's the golden liquid magnified, Ulf. The hexagonal shapes are cells from a phoenix.'

'From a phoenix?'

'They're phoenix tears, Ulf. I'm certain that's what this is. The tears of phoenixes were once used in potions on account of their life-giving properties. It would explain the change in the ghosts.'

Ulf was looking down the microscope, fascinated by the golden cells. New ones kept popping up in the solution, appearing as if from nowhere.

'What you can see are spontaneous stem cells coming to life, Ulf. They're unique in all of science. They're what enable phoenixes to regenerate their bodies and live many lifetimes, turning to flames then rising again from the ashes.'

Each tiny cell seemed to be bursting with energy, as if the golden liquid had a life of its own. 'It's weird,' Ulf said, looking up.

'A long time ago, people used phoenix tears to make themselves live longer or even bring themselves back from the brink of death,' Dr Fielding continued. She picked up a sample test tube from the rack. 'I'm surprised that the royal family would have used them, though.'

'How come?' Ulf asked.

'Because phoenix tears were obtained by cruelty, Ulf; the birds were made to cry.'

'The poor things,' Ulf said.

'The wild phoenix population didn't fully recover until Professor Farraway's time. The Professor set up a repopulation program, generating a colony of wild phoenixes from the DNA of just one bird.'

Ulf thought for a moment. He half-remembered having seen a picture of a phoenix somewhere at Farraway Hall. 'Was it a golden phoenix, Dr Fielding?' he asked.

'That's right, Ulf. The Professor had a Golden Fork-tailed Phoenix. It perched at Farraway Hall.'

She removed the glass slide from under the microscope and sat on the edge of the table. 'Well, it looks like we're finally getting on top of things here. The spectre's back safely and we know what this potion is now. I'm sure by tomorrow we'll have worked out where it came from.'

'By tomorrow?' Ulf asked.

'I'd like us to stay here tonight. It'll give me a chance to monitor how the living ghosts are adjusting to their bodies. I'll ask Zazz to fix us some beds. You can have the room Professor Farraway used to stay in, if you like.'

'Great,' Ulf said, excited. He couldn't wait to tell Tiana they were staying the night in the haunted castle. He crossed to the door. 'Dr Fielding, I think the ghosts like having their bodies back. They seem quite happy about it.'

'That's how it seems to me, too,' Dr Fielding replied. 'It must be exciting to have a second chance at life.'

CHAPTER FIFTEEN

That evening, Ulf and Tiana ate their supper in the truck: sausages for Ulf and honey for Tiana. Ulf told the fairy that Harold was now safely back in the Quarantine Room, and about how Dr Fielding had solved the mystery of the ghosts coming to life – that a potion of phoenix tears had caused it. 'You were right,' he confessed. 'Nothing bad is going on.'

The fairy paid little attention. She was too busy fretting that they were going to be spending the night in a castle full of ghosts.

When they'd finished eating, Zazz showed them to their sleeping quarters, opening the door to a royal bedchamber.

'Is it haunted, Zazz?' Tiana asked.

'Only by fright-mites. But hopefully they won't bother you. I've sprayed the bed with ghost repellent,' Zazz replied.

Ulf stepped into the room. It had a four-poster bed, a writing desk and a balcony overlooking the courtyard. The walls and ceiling were wriggling with tiny black shadows – the whole room was infested with fright-mites, fleeting emotions left over from unsettled lives.

'They don't bite, do they?' Tiana asked, glancing around nervously.

'That depends if they're hungry,' Zazz replied. He smiled. 'Sweet dreams.' And with a flash and a puff of smoke, he disappeared.

Ulf brushed the dust from a silk cushion on the bed. 'Here, Tiana, you can sleep on this.'

Ulf looked around the room and imagined Professor Farraway staying here years ago, studying the ghosts. The Professor had probably worked at that desk in the corner, he thought, and slept in this very bed.

Ulf went out on to the balcony. The rain had stopped and a crescent moon shone above Howling Forest. He could see ghost knights on the castle's walls and, down in the courtyard, he could make out Orson's boots poking from the stables. The giant was settling down to sleep.

Ulf heard snoring close by. He glanced to his left and saw Druce the gargoyle perched on the balcony's edge, turned to stone. 'Tiana, Druce is here,' he whispered.

Tiana was jumping on the cushion, flattening its bumps. 'Oh no, that's all we need, a snoring gargoyle.'

Ulf looked out over Howlhammer, thinking about everything that had happened that day: the ghosts coming to life, the escaped prisoner and the discovery of the phoenix tears. Suddenly, he remembered where he'd seen the picture of the golden phoenix. It was in the Gallery of Science. It was the picture the Professor's ghost had written his message on!

'Ulf, are you coming in?' the little fairy called.

Ulf's mind began racing. It can't have been a coincidence, he thought. The Professor had shown him that picture on purpose. 'Tiana, the Professor wrote his message on a picture of a phoenix,' he said.

'So?'

'So, first a prisoner goes missing, then Dr Fielding finds phoenix tears here. The Professor *was* warning us about Howlhammer, Tiana. Something bad *is* going on here. I'm sure of it.'

'Ulf, stop worrying,' Tiana replied. 'Nothing's the matter here except you, silly.'

Ulf heard Druce gurgle beside him. He saw the gargoyle open one eye. 'Phoenix was my friend,' Druce said.

'Pardon, Druce?'

The gargoyle had turned from stone to flesh. 'Professor's phoenix was Drucey's friend. Played on roof with Drucey.' The gargoyle's mouth drooped sadly. 'Professor went, then phoenix went too.' Druce flapped his stubby little wings. 'Fly away, phoenix, fly away, friend.' He leapt from the balcony, pretending to fly like a bird.

A moment later Ulf heard a gurgled cry. 'Blaargh!'

He peered over the edge of the balcony and saw Druce tangled in creepers below. 'Druce, are you okay?' he called down.

The gargoyle giggled. 'Oops! Drucey crash.'

'Be quiet out there, Ulf, or you'll wake everyone,' Tiana called.

Ulf went inside to talk to her. He was still thinking about the picture of the phoenix and the warning the Professor had written on it. 'Tiana, I'm sure it's not just a coincidence,' he said.

The fairy sighed. 'Ulf, go to bed.'

But Ulf paced back and forth. 'The prisoner is more dangerous than you think,' he said. 'What was he warning us about? There *must* be something dangerous about Harold.'

'Ulf, Harold's only a ghost,' Tiana replied. 'He's back now, and he hasn't even got a head. He's *not* dangerous.'

Ulf didn't feel so sure. 'None of the other ghosts like him, Tiana, the King least of all.'

Ulf thought back to what he'd read in *The Book of Beasts* – to know a ghost's intentions, you must first know its past. He crossed to the door.

'Ulf, where are you going?'

'To find out about Harold,' he said. 'I'm going to speak to the King.'

CHAPTER SIXTEEN

Ulf crept into Dr Fielding's workroom. She was up late, tapping notes into her laptop computer. Ulf glanced around, looking for the ghost canister containing the ghost of the King. He saw it standing in the corner.

Dr Fielding looked up from her computer. 'Ulf, what are you doing up?' she asked.

On her desk Ulf saw the rack with the test tubes containing samples of the phoenix tears from the ghosts. He stepped close beside her. 'I couldn't sleep,' he said. 'I thought I'd come and see what you were doing.' Ulf sneakily reached behind her and lifted a test tube from the rack. He slipped it into his back pocket.

'I'm just writing up my case notes, Ulf,' Dr Fielding replied. 'You should be in bed.'

'Oh, I suppose you're right. Goodnight then,' he said, and he shuffled backwards towards the door. As Dr Fielding began typing her notes again, Ulf tiptoed to the corner of the room, picked up the ghost canister and crept out, closing the door behind him.

Tiana was hovering in the corridor outside. 'Ulf, what have you got there?' she asked suspiciously.

'Shhh,' Ulf whispered, creeping away down the dark corridor. He shone his torch along the stone floor, following Harold's muddy bootprints to the spot where the King had been sucked up. Ulf saw the King's crown and sword at the side of the corridor. He placed the canister on the floor beside them and turned its nozzle. A hissing sound came from it.

'Ulf, what are you doing?' Tiana asked.

Ulf heard moaning and groaning as the ghost of King Stephen seeped from the canister. He saw the sword and the crown float up into the air. Next, he took the test tube of phoenix tears from his pocket and flicked a few drops towards the sword and crown. The golden droplets hung in mid-air as if floating. Then, around each one, Ulf saw parts of a body forming – a hand appeared, then an arm, a shoulder and a red robe. The King was coming back to life, his body solidifying.

'Oh, Ulf, what have you done!' Tiana cried. 'Dr Fielding will be furious.'

Ulf saw King Stephen's face appear, looking surprised. The King felt his body. 'I'm alive!' he said. He looked down at Ulf. 'Thank you.'

'Your Majesty, I need your help,' Ulf told him.

'Who are you?' the King asked.

'I'm Ulf, from the RSPCB.'

'And he's going to be in *big* trouble,' Tiana added.

'Your Majesty, there's something I need to know,' Ulf continued. 'Who was Headless Harold?'

The King's expression turned serious.

'Harold – that villain! He was the leader of an enemy army,' the King said, raising his sword in anger. 'The most ruthless army of cut-throats and thieves ever to have darkened this land. Harold led them to Howlhammer to wage war against me.' He swished his sword through the air. 'Harold wanted to be king!'

Ulf stepped back, seeing the King becoming more agitated. 'And what happened?' he asked.

'A battle, a most terrible and bloody battle,' the King replied. 'My knights and I rode out and surprised Harold's army before they reached the castle. We defeated them – left them for dead on the battlefield. It was an ugly sight: hundreds of dead soldiers, and the ground stained red with their blood.'

'And Harold? What about him?'

'Harold was brought back to the castle and thrown into the prison tower. He was put on trial then executed, his head chopped off. His ghost has haunted the castle ever since, and as long as it does I shall not rest in peace.'

Ulf thought for a moment. 'So Harold wanted to be king,' he said.

Tiana circled Ulf's head. 'What does it matter, Ulf? That was all in the past.'

Ulf shone his torch down the corridor on to Harold's muddy bootprints. 'Your Majesty, did you say the battlefield was stained red?'

'Blood red,' the King replied.

Harold's muddy bootprints were red too.

'Harold's been back there,' Ulf said.

'To the battlefield? But why?' the King asked.

Ulf paced up and down, thinking hard. 'The prisoner is more dangerous than you think,' he muttered. He turned to Tiana. 'Harold *is* dangerous, Tiana. He's got an army.'

Tiana giggled. 'Ulf, Harold's army's dead.'

Ulf glanced at the test tube of phoenix tears in his hand. 'So was Harold until yesterday,' he said. He looked up at the King. 'Your Majesty, could you show me the way to the battlefield?'

'Do you think Harold's been up to something?' the King asked.

'I think we should hurry,' Ulf replied. 'I'll meet you both by the castle gates in five minutes.'

'Ulf, this is crazy,' Tiana said.

Ulf crept away down the corridor; there was something he wanted from the Potions Room.

CHAPTER SEVENTEEN

Meanwhile, in Howling Forest, two tractor headlights shone in the darkness, lighting the muddy ground.

Baron Marąckai stepped from the shadows, holding Harold's head. 'It's time to begin, Harold,' he whispered. Then he called out, 'Blud, Bone, to business!'

Blud hurried over from the trailer carrying a watering can, and Bone came lumbering behind him with a large wooden crate. Bone placed the crate on the muddy ground beside the Baron. The crate had a tap on its front and a dial on its side. The dial was marked from one to two-hundred volts.

'Now what, Sir?' Bone asked.

'Just turn it on,' the Baron ordered.

Bone slowly turned the dial on the side of the crate: ten volts – there was a buzzing sound of electricity; twenty volts – the dial began sparking; fifty volts – from inside the crate came squawks; one-hundred volts – then screeches...

'Blud, get ready,' the Baron ordered.

Blud placed the watering can under the tap at the front of the crate.

Two-hundred volts – the squawks and screeches grew louder. Golden liquid began trickling from the tap.

The Baron grinned. 'Fill it all the way, Blud.'

When the watering can was full, Bone turned the dial on the crate to zero. The buzzing and squawks quietened and the golden liquid stopped trickling.

'Now sprinkle it on the mud, Blud,' the Baron ordered.

Blud looked puzzled. 'On the mud? What for, Sir? Is it for the mud monster?'

'Just do as I tell you!' the Baron spat. 'Then come back for a refill.'

'Yes, Sir. Right away, Sir,' Blud replied. He picked up the watering can and stepped through the trees, sprinkling the golden liquid on the muddy ground.

The Baron held up Harold's head to watch. The mud glistened as the golden liquid oozed into it. The ground began trembling.

'S-s-something's h-h-happening, Sir,' Blud called.

'Don't stop,' the Baron ordered.

The mud was moving. It bubbled and squelched as if something was stirring beneath it.

Blud came running back. 'Sir, I don't like this. What's down there?'

'Just keep sprinkling,' the Baron said.

But Blud was staring at the ground, horrified. Bony fingers were poking through the mud. Skeletal hands were pushing upwards. 'What's going on?' Blud asked. He hid with Bone behind a tree. 'I'm frightened.'

More hands reached up from underground: dozens of them, wherever the liquid had been sprinkled. They were clawing and scrabbling at the mud. Arms began appearing, then heads, as rotten corpses heaved themselves up.

'My army,' Harold said, amazed. 'They're alive!'

The Baron smiled. 'And they shall fight again, Harold.'

CHAPTER EIGHTEEN

Ulf crept across the dark courtyard to the castle gates. He could hear Orson snoring in the stables and the clip-clop of hooves. King Stephen was leading a unicorn past the sleeping giant. It was the huge stallion beast that Ulf had groomed earlier.

The King led it closer.

'Are we going by unicorn?' Ulf whispered.

'It'll be faster,' the King replied. 'The battlefield's about two miles west of here.' The King climbed up on to the unicorn's back, then reached down and pulled Ulf up behind him.

Tiana was perched on the unicorn's horn. 'We're going to be in so much trouble if Dr

Fielding finds out about this, Ulf,' she said.

The King gestured to a ghost knight and the knight quietly opened the castle gate. 'Hold tight,' the King instructed, and he tapped his heels against the unicorn's sides.

Ulf gripped the King's waist as the beast lurched forwards and galloped out of the castle then down the hill into Howling Forest. Ulf was juddering up and down on the unicorn's back, branches and leaves whipping his face. Tiana sparkled to light the way.

'The battle took place on Biggles Moor,' the King said. 'From Rover's Ridge to the Black River crossing.'

The unicorn's hooves pounded the ground as it carried them further and further into Howling Forest. In the moonlight, Ulf saw a stream winding alongside them.

'My knights and I came this way,' the King said.

The unicorn leapt over a fallen tree and galloped through the stream, water splashing up over Ulf.

'Then we took a short cut through Gater's Gulley.' The King tugged the unicorn's reins and the beast veered out of the stream and into a tunnel of trees. 'We met them at the gulley's end. That's where the worst bloodshed took place.'

As the King spoke, Ulf heard voices from up ahead. Through the tunnel of trees, he noticed lights.

'The battlefield is directly ahead of us now,' the King said.

'Slow down, Your Majesty. I think there's someone there.'

The King slowed the unicorn to a trot.

Ulf could make out figures moving among the trees. 'Your Majesty, I don't like the look of this,' he whispered. 'We should keep out of sight.'

The King brought the unicorn to a standstill and they dismounted. 'Stay,' the King whispered in the stallion's ear.

The unicorn seemed to understand. It stayed back as they crept through the trees trying to see who was there. Ulf's bare feet were squelching through mud. He glanced down and saw the mud was red – *blood* red. As he got nearer, he saw the lights were the headlights of a tractor. Ulf could make out figures carrying swords and shields.

'Soldiers!' he whispered. 'Dim your sparkles, Tiana.'

The fairy stopped sparkling to keep from being seen.

Ulf hid behind a tree. There were soldiers everywhere, lots of them, filling the forest. 'It's Harold's army. They're alive!'

'But how can this be?' the King asked, shocked. 'My knights and I killed them all.'

Ulf stayed low and crawled nearer, still keeping out of sight. There was a soldier just a few metres away. Bones were sticking out from under his tunic, half of his face was hanging off and one eye was dangling from his skull. Ulf saw another soldier dragging his leg, the foot missing, and another with only one arm. They were drooling and groaning, their bodies part bone and part rotting flesh.

'They're zombies!' Ulf said.

CHAPTER NINETEEN

'Soldierssss! Into formation!' a voice hissed loudly.

Ulf watched as the zombies staggered through the trees and lined up in rows, shoulder to rotten shoulder. There were hundreds of them.

'Eyessss front!' the voice ordered.

'I know that voice. It's Harold,' the King whispered, crouching beside Ulf.

Tiana hovered between them. 'But Harold's in the castle, isn't he?' she said.

Ulf peered through the branches to where the voice had come from. Over the heads of the zombie army, in the glare of the tractor's headlights, he glimpsed a severed head held aloft. 'It's Harold's head!' he said.

'Soldiersssssss, lisssssssten carefully!' Harold's head ordered. 'Tonight we march on Howlhammer Cassstle! And thisssss time, victory will be oursssss.'

'Ug! Ug! Ug!' the zombie soldiers cheered.

'And when the battle issss won, I will be King and you shall eat the loserssssss!'

The zombies shook their weapons: 'Ug! Ug! Ug!'

Ulf stared in horror, fearing for his friends back at the castle; Orson, Dr Fielding and Druce were in danger!

The King rested his hand on Ulf's shoulder. 'I must alert my knights immediately. It's our only hope.'

'Go, Your Majesty. Prepare your defences,' Ulf whispered. 'There's something I need to do here.'

The King nodded then stepped back through the trees towards Gater's Gully.

'Ulf, why are you sticking around?' Tiana asked.

Ulf was squinting in the direction of Harold's head. A hand was holding it above the army. He could see the fur-trimmed cuff of a sleeve. 'This way, Tiana,' he whispered, creeping around the army to get a closer look. He crouched behind a tree a few metres from the front line of zombie soldiers and peered into the glare of the tractor's headlights. Holding Harold's head was a tall man in a long fur coat with a face that was twisted like a rotten apple core… 'Marackai!' Ulf said. He looked at the fairy. 'Tiana, it's him. It's Marackai.'

The fairy gasped, seeing the beast hunter. 'What's *he* doing here? I thought he was dead!'

Marackai was walking along the front line of zombie soldiers with Harold's head in his hand, inspecting their weapons.

'I don't like this, Ulf,' Tiana said, sounding frightened.

Just then, Ulf heard a squawk. He turned and, through the trees, saw the Baron's henchmen, Blud and Bone holding a watering can under the tap of a wooden crate. Squawks and screeches were coming from inside the crate and golden liquid was trickling from a tap on its front. 'Phoenix tears…' Ulf muttered.

Bone turned a dial on the side of the crate and the squawks and screeches stopped, then the two men walked off sprinkling the golden liquid on to the ground. Ulf saw more zombies pushing their way up from the mud. 'Quick, Tiana, follow me,' he whispered.

Keeping to the shadows, Ulf dashed from tree to tree, and hid beside the crate. Quietly he pushed its lid open a crack. 'Shine your sparkles inside, Tiana.'

The fairy flew in and began to glow. 'It's a phoenix!' she cried.

By the light of the fairy's sparkles, Ulf saw a phoenix in the crate bound in a leather harness. It had golden feathers and a forked tail. 'It's the Professor's phoenix,' he said. 'Marackai's extracting its tears.'

There was a leather helmet pulled over the bird's head with tubes running from two eyeholes to the tap at the crate's front. Ulf saw

the tubes were full of golden tears. In the corner of the crate was a large battery with lots of wires coming from it that were pushed under the bird's feathers.

'Ulf, he's torturing it! He's making it cry!' Tiana said. She darted down to the bird and started tugging on the wires.

'Free it, Tiana,' Ulf said. 'I'll be back in a minute.'

'Ulf, where are you going?'

He glanced over at the zombie army. 'I'm going to stop Marackai. This is *his* evil work.'

'But, Ulf, he'll kill you!'

'No, he won't.' Ulf took out a bottle of silver liquid from his pocket and showed it to the fairy. 'I've got this.'

'Moonjuice!' Tiana exclaimed.

'I found it in the Potions Room,' Ulf told her. 'I'm going to show Marackai some wolf strength!'

The little fairy tugged on another wire. 'Go, Ulf. Transform and tear him to pieces!'

Ulf smiled then closed the lid on the crate.

With the moonjuice in his hand he crept round the back of the tractor and trailer. He took a deep breath and ran out to face the Baron. 'Marackai, the game's up!' he called.

Ulf saw zombie soldiers looking at him. Baron Marackai stepped forwards, holding Harold's head. The Baron looked at Ulf, surprised. 'Well, well, well. It seems we have a spy in our camp,' he said.

'It's over, Marackai!' Ulf told him. He held up the bottle of moonjuice. 'I'm here to stop you.'

'Who isssss thissss boy?' Harold's head hissed.

'I'm not a boy,' Ulf said. 'I'm a werewolf.' He pulled the cork from the moonjuice and glugged the silver liquid, feeling it running coolly down his throat. Ulf licked his lips and braced himself for his wolf transformation.

The Baron grinned. 'You think you're so clever, don't you, werewolf?'

'I've seen the phoenix,' Ulf said. 'I know you've been torturing it for its tears.'

'Well, I needed them to bring Harold and his army back from the dead. Oh, and I had a little fun with the ghosts too, to lure you and your do-gooder friends to the castle.' The Baron smiled. 'Don't you see, werewolf? Harold and his army want revenge and, thanks to my genius, they will get it. They will destroy Howlhammer Castle and everyone in it – including your friends.'

'I'll tear you to pieces first,' Ulf said.

But the Baron merely laughed. 'You can't kill me, werewolf. I have my father's phoenix, remember. Its tears have been keeping me alive for years.'

Ulf was still waiting for his transformation to start. Why was it taking so long? He felt a pain in his stomach. Then a wave of nausea overcame him and he started sweating.

'Feel a bit ill do you, werewolf?'

Ulf clutched his stomach. He was in agony. What was happening to him?

The Baron stepped forwards and shoved Ulf to the ground, pressing on Ulf's chest with his serpent-skin boot. 'You stupid werewolf. You fell for my little trick.' The Baron snatched the empty bottle from Ulf's hand. 'While I was in the castle, I paid a visit to the Potions Room and swapped the royal moonjuice for a poisonous concoction of my own: mercury and arsenic.'

Poison! Ulf thought. He could feel his throat tightening. He was becoming weak.

The Baron reached into his pocket and took out a second bottle of silver liquid. '*This* is the one you meant to drink,' he said, grinning. 'Oh dear, and now you're going to die.'

Ulf felt dizzy. His arms and legs felt numb.

The Baron leaned down, sneering at him, and pressed the bottle of real moonjuice into Ulf's hand. 'Want a sip, do you?'

But Ulf couldn't move. He was paralysed. The poison was taking effect.

'Oh dear, can't you drink it? Too weak, are you?' The Baron laughed. 'Ha ha haaa ha haaaaa! Well, look on the bright side: at least you won't die all hairy.'

Baron Marackai stepped back, smiling, then glanced up at the sky – the first rays of dawn were breaking through the trees. 'OH, WHAT A BEAUTIFUL MORNING TO WIPE THE RSPCB FROM THE EARTH,' he said. 'Sorry to have to leave you dying, werewolf, but now I'm off to kill your friends too.'

The Baron held Harold's head aloft. 'Right then, Harold, shall we go?'

Harold's head grinned. 'Soldiersss, onwardsss to the cassstle!' he ordered. 'Forwardsss maaarch!'

'Ug! Ug! Ug!'

Ulf heard the zombies cheer, then a numbness took hold of him and everything went black.

CHAPTER TWENTY

Tiana heard the roar of engines and the tramping of feet. She felt the crate jolt, and peered out through a small crack in its side. It was being lifted off the ground; the zombie army was on the move. Where's Ulf? she thought.

She was hurriedly struggling to free the phoenix. The bird was limp with exhaustion, and squawked feebly from under its mask. 'Hang in there,' Tiana said to it.

The electric wires were taking forever to disconnect. To the little fairy, each felt as thick and heavy as steel cable. Sometimes they'd spark and send her jolting backwards. She disconnected the last of them, then wiped sweat from her forehead and began tackling the harness that was holding the bird's body. The harness was made from leather straps buckled across the phoenix's wings and around its neck. Tiana began pushing the loose end of a strap back through its metal buckle. Then she strained and tugged, heaving the strap over the buckle's pin. 'One done,' she said.

The phoenix shook its wing and squawked.

One by one, Tiana undid each of the straps around the phoenix's wings and body and, as each strap loosened, the phoenix regained a little more movement.

She heard the bird caw.

'I'll get you out,' she said. 'Trust me.'

Tiana flew to the leather helmet fastened around the bird's head. Running up the back of the helmet was a zip. 'Put your head down a little,' she whispered.

The phoenix tilted its head forwards and Tiana pulled the zip fastener, dragging it up. There was a slow clicking sound as it moved. With both hands, and trying not to slip on the leather, she dragged the zip open. She pulled on the tubes attached to the mask and, as the mask came off, tears from the tubes spurted all over her, drenching her from head to toe in golden liquid. She shook herself, then looked at the bird's eyes. They were bloodshot and rimmed with a golden crust where it had been crying. It blinked. 'It's time to go now,' she said to it. 'You're free.'

The phoenix puffed up its feathers and flapped its wings, but when it tried to fly it couldn't. Its legs were secured by a metal chain to a ring in the floor of the crate.

'Drat,' Tiana said. 'Okay, brace yourself. This one calls for some heat.'

The fairy flew down and shot her sparkles towards the chain like a blowtorch. 'Keep still. I don't want to burn you,' she said to the phoenix.

The metal chain began heating up and started to glow. 'Now, on the count of three, I want you to flap your wings again. One…'

The chain glowed white hot.

'Two…'

Its metal was softening.

'Three!'

The phoenix flapped its wings and rose a little, pulling on the chain. A link in the chain began bending.

'Harder!' Tiana said.

The bird kept flapping.

'Keep going!'

The chain snapped and the bird flew upwards, bursting open the lid of the crate.

Tiana zoomed out after it, following the phoenix up into the trees. She saw it flying higher and higher, squawking with joy in the rays of the rising sun. 'That's it,' she called. 'Fly away from here, pretty bird!'

Then she glanced down and saw the crate trundling away on the sidecar of a motorbike. It was being carried off by the Baron's henchmen, the zombie army marching in a long line ahead of them through the forest. Floating in the sky above was a hot-air balloon heading for Howlhammer Castle.

Harold's voice was shouting from the balloon's basket: 'Left, right, left, right…'

The Baron and Harold's army were off to battle! Tiana had a sudden feeling of dread; Ulf hadn't managed to stop them, she realised. Where was he?

'Ulf?' she called, zooming back over the trees. 'Ulf, where are you?'

CHAPTER TWENTY-ONE

Ulf was dying. His eyes were shut and it was as if he was drifting through blackness. Faces and memories were rushing past him. He saw Orson smiling, carrying a sack of feed across the beast park. He saw Dr Fielding kneeling in the straw watching the hatching of a baby griffin. He saw Tiana chasing a bumblefly across the freshwater lake, and Druce pulling ugly faces on the rooftop of Farraway Hall. Then, ahead of him, he saw a speck of light. It was beckoning him on. Ulf could feel himself drifting towards it, getting closer and closer. The nearer he got, the larger the light appeared, until it was bright and round like a full moon.

'Don't die, Ulf,' he heard.

Ulf could feel himself slowing. He felt a tingling on his lips, then saw the big bright light shrinking again. He realised he was moving back from it, getting further away until it returned to just a tiny speck.

'Don't die, Ulf,' he heard again. It was Tiana's voice. 'You're my best friend in the whole world. Please don't die.'

Ulf could hear other sounds too: the wind howling and trees rustling. He woke, and found himself lying in the mud in Howling Forest. Tiana was perched on his chin dabbing his lips with golden liquid. She was soaked in the stuff.

'You're alive, Ulf! You're alive!' the fairy said, sparkling.

'What happened?' Ulf asked groggily.

'It's these phoenix tears, Ulf. They saved your life.' Tiana showed him her hands soaked in golden liquid.

Ulf sat up and looked around. In the dawn light he saw the forest was empty, the zombie army gone. 'Where's Marackai, Tiana?' he asked.

'He's leading the zombies to the castle,' Tiana replied.

'Then we have to stop him!'

'But how, Ulf?'

'With werewolf strength!' Ulf replied. He was still holding the bottle of real moonjuice that Marackai had used to taunt him. He pulled out its cork and glugged the moonjuice down.

Ulf's eyes flashed silver. A pain burst in the back of his neck and his spine began stretching. His bones grew as his skeleton realigned from biped to quadruped. He leapt on to all fours, thick dark hair spreading up his arms and over his body. His hands grew claws and his muscles expanded, ripping his T-shirt and jeans. Fangs split through his gums as his face twisted into that of a wolf. Ulf threw his head back and howled, 'Yaarooooo!'

Then he bounded off through the trees, heading for Howlhammer Castle.

CHAPTER TWENTY-TWO

'Dr Fielding, wake up!'

Dr Fielding lifted her head from the worktable. She rubbed her eyes and saw Zazz peering round the door. 'What's the matter?' she asked the genie.

'It's the King and his knights,' Zazz told her. 'Quick, come and see.'

Dr Fielding looked at her watch. It was five o'clock in the morning.

'Hurry,' Zazz said, and with genie power he whisked her downstairs to the courtyard.

'Knights, prepare for battle!' she heard. She saw King Stephen up on the top of the castle's outer wall, waving his sword.

'Oh my word. The King's come to life!' she said. 'How did this happen?'

'I don't know, Dr Fielding,' Zazz replied. 'And he's acting very strangely.'

The King was stationing his knights on the castle battlements. 'Swords ready!' he called. 'The enemy are approaching. Prepare to fight!'

From the stables, Orson looked out. 'Why's everyone awake?' he asked, yawning.

'It's okay, Orson, I'll deal with this,' Dr Fielding called. 'Come on, Zazz, let's get the King inside.'

But as Dr Fielding went to fetch the King, from outside the castle walls she heard the muffled tramp-tramp of marching feet. 'What's making that sound, Zazz?' she asked, stopping to listen.

Zazz flew up and looked over the high wall towards Howling Forest. 'Gadzooks!' the genie exclaimed. 'Dr Fielding, quick, come and see!'

Dr Fielding climbed the steps to the top of the castle wall and looked out over the battlements. 'Oh my goodness!' she said.

Marching through Howling Forest towards the castle were line upon line of soldiers. Above them, a hot-air balloon was floating in the dawn sky, a voice calling from it: 'Left, right, left, right.'

There were hundreds of soldiers, an entire army of them, wearing ragged clothes and rusted helmets, carrying swords and baseball bats, with some riding motorbikes.

'Halt!' the voice called from the hot-air balloon.

The army came to a standstill, and an eerie silence followed. In the dawn air Dr Fielding could smell the stench of rotten flesh.

Orson stepped over to see what was happening. 'Who are that lot?' he asked.

Dr Fielding stared, horrified, at the soldiers. She could see bones sticking from their clothes, and flesh hanging from them. 'Zombies!' she gasped.

Behind her Zazz swirled, frightened. 'Oh, Dr Fielding, what's going on?'

As the hot-air balloon drifted nearer, Dr Fielding gasped again seeing the man in its

basket. He was wearing a long fur coat. 'Marackai!'

The Baron was holding a severed head. King Stephen shook his sword at the balloon and called up from the battlements, 'Harold, you traitor!'

Orson looked up, puzzled. 'What's Marackai doing here?' he asked. 'I thought he was dead.'

'So did I,' Dr Fielding replied. 'I don't like the look of this.'

Baron Marackai called down, 'Residents of Castle Howlhammer, members of the RSPCB – PREPARE TO DIE!'

'Ug! Ug! Ug!' the zombies cheered.

'This day will go down in history,' the Baron called. 'This day will be remembered forever as the end of the RSPCB!'

'Soldierssss, get readyyy!' Harold's head called down.

The zombies stamped their feet and thrust their weapons in the air. 'Ug! Ug! Ug!'

The noise was deafening.

The castle walls shook.

'Soldierssss, attack!'

With a hideous snarling cry, the first line of zombie soldiers surged from the forest. A second line followed them, then a third. Wave after wave came charging at the castle.

'They've come to fight,' Orson said.

'Mercy help us,' Dr Fielding muttered. 'What are we going to do?' She looked down from the battlements. Zombies were climbing up the castle wall, gripping its crumbling stone with their bony hands.

'Need some help?' a little voice called.

Dr Fielding looked up in surprise as a tiny sparkle came zooming towards her. 'Tiana? How come you're— What are you—?'

'No time to explain,' Tiana said. 'I've brought reinforcements.' She pointed down into Howling Forest.

In the back lines of the zombie army Dr Fielding saw a commotion going on: zombies were being tossed into the air. A force was bursting through them, flinging them left and right. A loud howl rang out and Dr Fielding stared in amazement at a werewolf ploughing through the army, running at speed towards the castle.

'It's Ulf!' Orson said.

'He's transformed!' Tiana told them.

Ulf leapt on to the castle wall and began scaling it, clambering over the backs of the zombies, using them like a ladder. He pulled himself on to the battlements and stood panting beside Orson.

'Glad to see you, Ulf,' the giant said.

Dr Fielding looked bewildered. 'How—when—?'

'I'll tell you later,' Ulf growled. 'It's fighting time now.' He looked up at the hot-air balloon. 'Marackai, bring it on!'

CHAPTER TWENTY-THREE

Along the castle's battlements, zombie soldiers heaved themselves up, brandishing swords, baseball bats and chains, all of them gnashing their teeth hungrily.

'To battle!' Ulf roared. He leapt at a zombie and punched it clean off the wall, then ducked as another swiped at him with a rusty sword. He grabbed the zombie in his claws and hurled it from the battlements. Another zombie soldier swung at him with a baseball bat and he dodged, then ripped the bat from the zombie's hand, pulling off its bony arm too. He used the bat to whack the zombie, sending it flying. More zombies climbed up to attack. One swung a chain at Ulf, and Ulf bit it in two then did a roundhouse kick, knocking the zombie backwards. One by one he fought them off, hurling them back down to the forest below.

As Ulf fought, his friends fought too. Orson was picking zombies from the wall, tossing them away two at a time. 'We'll show them, Ulf,' the giant called.

Ulf saw King Stephen thrust his sword into a zombie and the blade come out of its back. The ghost knights were fighting bravely by the King's side, their swords swishing at dazzling speed, their armour protecting them.

Ulf saw Dr Fielding punch a zombie and its rotten head fall off. Tiana blasted zombies with her sparkles, and Zazz was zipping among them, snatching the weapons from their hands.

Howlhammer's defences were holding.

A voice shouted above the noise, 'You'll never win, werewolf! I've only just started!' It was Marackai calling from the hot-air balloon.

Baron Marackai held up Harold's head and

Harold shouted an order to his army, 'Zombiesssss! Attack the eassst wall!'

Ulf saw a line of zombies break off from the main army. He glanced to the east wall – it was unguarded.

On the main castle building Ulf saw Druce and the gargoyles blowing raspberries and pulling faces at the enemy.

'Druce, guard the east wall!' Ulf called.

'Gargoyles to battle! Follow Drucey!' Druce gurgled. He leapt to the top of the east wall, dozens of gargoyles bounding after him preparing to fight. As the zombies climbed on to the battlements, the gargoyles bashed them with their hard stony fists. 'Bluurgh! Blaaaargh!'

Ulf heard Baron Marackai's voice call from above. 'Oh, look, the ugly bunch are fighting too!'

Then the Baron held up Harold's head. 'Zombiesss, now attack the wessst wall!'

Another wave of zombies broke away from the main army, and Ulf glanced to the castle's west wall – it too was unguarded.

He bounded to Zazz, who was coiled around a zombie's throat. 'Zazz, we need reinforcements,' he said. 'Fetch the ghosts!'

With a flash and a puff of smoke, the genie disappeared. Then, moments later, the door of the main castle building burst open and Zazz came flying out with Poisoned Pete, The Hollow Admiral, The Duelling Duke, the Bubonic Maid, Frozen Nell, Tom the Target and even the Hungry Monk. The living ghosts were coming to join the battle too. The genie floated them up to the west wall just as the zombies reached its top.

'Take that!' the Duelling Duke cried, firing his pistol.

'Ha! Man overboard!' the Hollow Admiral laughed, pushing a zombie over the side of the wall.

'Fancy a drink?' Poisoned Pete asked, smashing a bottle over a zombie's head.

Ulf heard Baron Marackai shout, 'Still think you can stop me? Harold, send in more!'

'Cavalry, attack!' Harold's head ordered.

Ulf saw zombie soldiers laying wooden ramps at the foot of the castle. There was a roar of engines as zombies on motorbikes accelerated up them. The riders soared over the castle's outer wall and landed in the courtyard.

'Leave this one to me, Ulf,' King Stephen called. He put two fingers in his mouth and whistled.

On his whistle, the Howlhammer unicorns came galloping from the stable block into battle. They lowered their horns and charged at the zombie riders. The motorbikes were no match for the beasts. One by one the unicorns knocked the riders from their bikes, sending them skidding and crashing into the walls.

Everyone was fighting the zombies: ghosts, gargoyles, unicorns, knights and the RSPCB. And wherever the zombies tried to attack, they were beaten back.

Ulf glanced up at the hot-air balloon. 'Is that all you've got, Marackai?' he growled.

But Baron Marackai merely sneered. 'That's

just for starters, werewolf. Now it's time for my secret weapon.' He held up Harold's head.

'Do it now!' Harold ordered.

Secret weapon? What secret weapon? Ulf thought as he hurled another zombie off the battlements. He scanned the army below. What was Marackai talking about? Suddenly, Ulf felt a shiver run up his spine. He glanced to his left and saw Harold's headless body standing beside Orson. The spectre was clutching a sword.

'Hello, there. Come to help, have you?' the giant asked Harold.

'Orson, watch out!' Ulf called. 'Don't trust him!'

But Ulf's warning came too late, and he watched, horrified, as the spectre plunged the sword into Orson's boot.

'Yowzers!' the giant yelled, hopping on one leg clutching his foot in pain.

Harold's body ran at him, shoving Orson off-balance.

'Waaagh!' the giant called as he fell from the wall and landed with a thud on the hillside.

'No!' Ulf cried.

A bloodcurdling cheer rose from the zombie army, and dozens of zombie soldiers swarmed towards the dazed giant. At the same time, Harold lunged for Ulf, jabbing the sword in his arm.

Ulf staggered, bleeding, then with one paw he gripped Harold's body and flung it off the castle wall. A wave of zombies scrambled on to the battlements where the giant had been standing. They all charged at Ulf, bundling him backwards. Ulf crashed down into the courtyard, the zombies on top of him. They were drooling and gnashing their teeth. He could smell their rotting flesh. Then he heard the Baron jeer, 'It'll soon be over, werewolf.'

'Sssmash the gatessss!' Harold's head ordered.

THUMP! As Ulf struggled beneath the zombies, he heard something ram against the castle gates. He was trying to fight the zombies off, but they were pinning him down, biting him. One bit his leg, another his shoulder, another his tail. They were trying to eat him!

THUMP! The castle gates shuddered again. 'Defend the gates!' Ulf called.

THUMP! Ulf threw six zombies off him and saw the King and his knights racing down from the battlements. They pushed against the gates with their shoulders, trying to keep them closed, but the wooden bar holding the gates was bending and splintering.

THUMP! Ulf smashed two zombies together, then leapt on to all fours.

CRACK! The wooden bar holding the gates broke in two and Ulf saw Orson's head burst through. The zombie army was using the giant as a battering ram!

As Ulf ran to help the giant, CRASH! The gates smashed open and zombies flooded into the courtyard. **The castle had been breached.**

CHAPTER TWENTY-FOUR

A tide of zombies surged through the gates, forcing Ulf back. The whole of the zombie army was running into the courtyard at once. Orson was being trampled, lying unconscious on the ground. 'Ug! Ug! Ug!' the zombies roared.

Ulf ducked baseball bats and dodged swords, punched and kicked, trying to fight them, but more and more kept coming.

A shadow passed over him and Ulf looked up to see the Baron's hot-air balloon. The Baron was laughing. 'Ha ha haaaa ha haaaaaaaa! The RSPCB is finished!'

'Zombiessss, kill everyone!' Harold's head ordered.

As Ulf fought, he saw Zazz floating the ghosts down from the west wall to join the battle in the courtyard. The gargoyles leapt from the east wall to fight too. The Howlhammer unicorns were charging the zombies with their horns. Dr Fielding was fighting by the stable block, and the King and his knights were trying to defend the entrance. It was chaos. The battle was raging fiercely.

Ulf picked up a zombie in his claws and hurled it at another. Then he saw Druce in trouble: a zombie had hold of the gargoyle's tail and was swinging him round its head. Ulf bounded over the zombie army, using their heads like stepping-stones, racing to help.

'Drucey feeling sick!' the gargoyle gurgled, spinning round and round.

Ulf seized hold of Druce and pulled him free, ripping off the zombie's arms.

'Thanks, Fur Face,' Druce gurgled. He took the zombie's arms and started punching the zombie with them.

Ulf bashed zombies left and right, knocking

them across the courtyard. He saw the Hollow Admiral sword-fighting with one. The zombie thrust a sword at the Admiral and it went straight through the hole in the Admiral's stomach.

'Ha! Missed!' the Hollow Admiral said, bashing the zombie on the head.

Ulf saw Tiana blasting zombies with her sparkles, but one snatched the fairy from the air and popped her into its drooling mouth.

'No!' Ulf growled, bounding to save Tiana. He punched the zombie in the stomach and it doubled over, spitting the fairy back out.

'Yuck, what rotten breath!' Tiana said, shaking spit from her wings. She smiled at Ulf. 'Thanks,' she said. 'You saved my life.'

Ulf heard a splash behind him and saw a zombie ducking Frozen Nell headfirst into a barrel of water. He leapt over and pulled her out. 'Brrrr,' she shivered, spurting a mouthful of water. Ulf picked up the barrel, smashed it over the zombie's head, then charged back into battle.

Harold's head shouted from the hot-air balloon, 'Zombiesss, kill the King! Kill him! Do it nooooow!'

Ulf saw zombies swarming towards the King and his knights. As the knights tried to defend the King, the zombies tore at the knights' armour, flinging it in the air.

'Ug! Ug! Ug! Gill der Ging! Gill der Ging!'

'Get me hisss crown!' Harold's head ordered. 'I'm to be King! Revenge isss mine!'

King Stephen was swiping at the zombies with his sword, but he was outnumbered.

As Ulf rushed to help, a zombie motorbike rider came speeding towards him. Ulf stepped on to the motorbike's front wheel and did a somersault over the handlebars. He landed on the seat behind the zombie rider and pushed the rider off, then he skidded the bike round and twisted the throttle, speeding towards the King.

The King was struggling under a pile of zombies. Ulf saw one of them throw the King's sword up to the basket of the balloon.

The zombies cheered, 'Ug! Ug! Ug!'

'Now hisss crown!' Harold hissed.

Ulf saw the zombies toss up the King's crown. They cheered again, 'Ug! Ug! Ug!'

Ulf pulled the bike up into a wheelie. A zombie lunged for him but Ulf turned the handlebars, whacking the zombie sideways. Then he saw a zombie opening its mouth, about to bite the king's ear. Ulf reached down, grabbing the zombie by its hair and yanking it away. Then he pulled the King on to the back of the bike and rode in a tight circle, knocking the zombies down like skittles.

'Thank you, Ulf,' King Stephen said as they sped away through the army. 'When this is over, you must teach me how to ride one of these.'

The King reached out from the moving bike and snatched a zombie's sword, then leapt from the bike on to a galloping unicorn and charged back into battle.

Ulf heard Baron Marackai call down, 'Think you're a hero, do you, werewolf? Well, you can't save everyone.'

Ulf saw a rope with a metal hook on its end lowering from the balloon's basket.

'Pass her up,' the Baron called. He pulled on the rope and Ulf saw Dr Fielding being lifted from the battle zone. She was gagged and wrapped in chains, struggling to free herself.

'Nooo!' Ulf growled, rushing to save her.

'Too slow, werewolf!' the Baron sneered. He bundled Dr Fielding into the balloon's basket then fired the burner.

Ulf looked up helplessly as the hot-air balloon rose into the air, taking Dr Fielding away.

*　　*　　*

As the hot-air balloon gained height, the Baron picked up the crown from the floor of the basket. 'Oh, how pretty,' he said, watching it glint in the morning light.

'Mine at lasssst,' Harold's head said. 'Put it on me.'

Baron Marackai admired the crown. 'Shiny, isn't it, Harold?'

'Hurrrrry up,' Harold demanded. 'I've been waiting over fiiive hundred yearsssss for that crown.'

The Baron polished the crown with the sleeve of his coat. 'Oooh, look at how gold it is.'

'Come on, we had an agreement: I get to be Kiing and you get to dessstroy the RSsssPCB.'

'Ah yes, about that… I lied,' the Baron replied. He placed the crown on his own head and smiled. 'I HEREBY DECLARE MYSELF KING MARACKAI THE FIRST OF HOWLHAMMER.'

Harold's face turned angry. 'But—'

The Baron merely laughed. 'Goodbye, Harold,' he said, and he threw the head over the side of the basket.

'Aaaaaaaaaagh,' Harold's head cried, plummeting to the courtyard below.

The Baron adjusted the crown then looked to the floor of the basket where Dr Fielding was wrapped in chains. He placed his serpent-skin boot on her chest. 'Well, Dr Fielding, what shall I do with you?'

With her mouth gagged, she could barely

speak, 'Hrghmmm nghhhh nghhh,' she groaned, struggling.

'Pardon?' the Baron said, kneeling down next to her. 'Did you say you'd like to watch your friends die then have me execute you with this?' From the floor of the basket he picked up the King's sword. 'Why, certainly, it would be my pleasure.'

CHAPTER TWENTY-FIVE

Ten zombie soldiers came charging towards Ulf. He saw the Baron's henchmen, Blud and Bone, riding alongside them in a motorbike and sidecar.

'That's the one,' Blud said, pointing at him.

The zombies encircled Ulf. They were drooling hungrily, licking their rotten teeth. All at once, they lunged for him, their jaws gnashing and their bony hands grasping. 'Ug! Ug! Ug!' They pinned Ulf's arms to his sides.

'Hold him still,' Bone said. The big man jumped from the sidecar with a long metal chain and wrapped it around Ulf's body.

Blud sniggered from the bike. 'There's no

point in struggling, werewolf. You're for it now.'

Ulf felt the chain tightening and the zombies overpowering him, their teeth gnashing hungrily.

Summoning all his wolf strength, Ulf flexed his muscles and pushed his arms against the chain. Power surged through him and, in a roaring explosion, he snapped the chain into pieces, sending the zombies flying.

He snarled at Blud and Bone. 'If you want me, get me yourselves.'

'You do it, Bone. He looks angry,' Blud said nervously.

Bone picked up a piece of the broken chain and swung it at Ulf. Ulf grabbed it in his claws and ripped it from the big man's grip.

Bone glanced at Blud. 'Now what?'

Ulf bared his fangs and growled at the two men. Bone's knees trembled. 'Let's get out of here!' he cried. He dived into the motorbike's sidecar. Blud twisted the throttle and they sped away, weaving through the battle then fleeing through the castle gates.

'Come back, you cowards!' Ulf heard from above. He looked up and saw the Baron's hot-air balloon on the roof of the castle. Marackai was stepping out of its basket, shaking his fist. He shouted down at Ulf, 'You still won't beat me, werewolf! I'm King now – King Marackai of Howlhammer!'

Ulf saw the Baron had the King's crown on his head.

The Baron dragged Dr Fielding from the balloon's basket and raised the King's sword. 'From this day forth, the RSPCB is officially abolished!' he shouted.

The battle was raging all around. With the castle's outer defences breached, the sheer number of zombies was overwhelming.

Tiana flew to Ulf's side. 'We can't hold out much longer,' she cried. 'What are we going to do, Ulf? The zombies will kill us all!'

Ulf tried to think. He saw zombie soldiers marauding in the courtyard. Zazz was lifting one into the air using genie power. Then he saw Druce on the castle wall holding a severed head. The gargoyle was licking it and blowing raspberries in its face. It was *Harold's* head, Ulf realised. Ulf had an idea. 'Tiana, there may be a way we can win,' he said.

'How, Ulf?' Tiana asked desperately.

'Listen carefully.' Ulf whispered his plan and the fairy smiled. 'Tell Druce – and Zazz too.'

The fairy zoomed off. 'I'll do my best, Ulf. Good luck.'

Ulf bounded on all fours to the main castle building. He leapt up and started scaling its sheer front, clawing his way up the crumbling stone. He climbed up creepers and over balconies, heading higher, then pulled himself on to the rooftop. He saw the Baron pressing the tip of the King's sword to Dr Fielding's throat.

'Let her go, Marackai,' Ulf called.

The Baron swung the sword towards Ulf. 'Don't you ever give up, werewolf? I'm King now. I give the orders around here.' The Baron jabbed his sword at Ulf, and Ulf dodged. The Baron attacked again, slashing the sword back and forth. Ulf ducked and dodged, the blade only narrowly missing him. The Baron forced Ulf backwards until he felt himself standing at the very edge of the rooftop.

The Baron raised the sword above his head. 'IT'S TIME TO DIE, WEREWOLF!'

'I don't think so,' Ulf growled.

There was a flash then a puff of purple smoke, and the sword disappeared from Baron Marackai's hand. The Baron stepped back, startled. 'What the—'

'Thanks, Zazz,' Ulf called, looking up. The genie was floating high in the air above the castle, the sword safely in his grasp.

'Give up now, Marackai,' Ulf snarled. 'Or face the consequences.'

The Baron sneered. 'Consequences? What consequences, werewolf? You're too late – nothing can stop the zombies now.'

'Oh, yeah?' Ulf growled. He glanced towards a nearby turret. On its top sat Druce, holding Harold's head. Tiana was hovering in front of it.

She kicked Harold in the nose. 'Say it!'

'Say it, Haroldy!' Druce gurgled.

'But—'

Tiana pulled Harold's nostril hairs as hard as she could and Druce poked his tongue in Harold's ear. 'Say it!'

'Kill the King,' Harold mumbled.

'Louder!' Tiana said.

'Kill the King,' Harold repeated.

'Louder!' Druce gurgled.

'KILL THE KING!' Harold shouted. 'KILL THE KING! KILL THE KING!'

The noise of the battle quietened and a puzzled silence filled the air as the zombies looked up from the courtyard.

Ulf faced the Baron. 'Nice crown you have there,' he snarled.

Marackai nervously touched the crown on his head. He looked down over the rooftop's edge.

'Ug! Ug! Ug!' Zombies began climbing up the castle building, drooling and gnashing their teeth. 'Gill der Ging! Gill der Ging!'

'Your reign is over, Marackai,' Ulf growled.

The zombies were clambering on to the roof: 'Gill der Ging,' they groaned. 'Gill der Ging.'

'No, there's been a misunderstanding!' Marackai cried, staggering backwards. 'You're not supposed to kill *me*!'

But the zombies paid no attention. They approached the Baron, drooling and hungry.

The Baron rushed to the hot-air balloon and dived into its basket. Zombies charged after him, scrabbling to get in too. 'Get away, you revolting creatures!' The Baron threw the crown at them and fired up the burner. The balloon began to rise, zombies clinging to its basket.

Ulf watched as the balloon floated high into the sky, the Baron trying to bash the zombies as they clawed at his fur coat. Ulf heard the Baron scream, 'I'll be back, werewolf. I'll get you if it's the last thing I doooooo!'

Ulf knelt beside Dr Fielding and bit through the chains around her, then pulled the gag from her mouth.

'Ulf, you saved us!' she said, giving him a hug.

He looked down to the courtyard and saw that no one was fighting; the zombies were all staring up at the balloon, watching it disappear into the clouds, the Baron's screams fading with it. Then Ulf heard Headless Harold's voice, 'Soldiersss sssurrender, lay down your weaponsss!'

Tiana was pulling Harold's ear. Druce licked the spectre's face. 'Good head,' he gurgled.

The zombie soldiers dropped their swords and baseball bats. Ulf saw knights gathering around Orson and helping him to his feet. The giant rubbed his head, then looked up at Ulf and gave a thumbs up. 'Looks like I missed all the fun, Ulf,' he called.

Ulf smiled, pleased to see that Orson was okay. He saw King Stephen on the back of the large stallion unicorn, raising his sword.

'Three cheers for the werewolf,' the King announced.

The courtyard erupted in celebration. The knights applauded, clanking their armour; the gargoyles gurgled, leaping for joy; the unicorns neighed, rearing up on their hind legs; and the ghosts all cheered, 'Hip hip, hooray. Hip hip, hooray. Hip hip, hooray!'

Even the zombies joined in, 'Ug! Ug! Uray!'

Ulf heard birdsong ring out. Perched on the top of the prison tower, he saw the phoenix, its golden feathers shining in the morning sun. He threw his head back and howled…

CHAPTER TWENTY-SIX

Ulf was woken by a gentle juddering. He opened his eyes and saw he was wrapped in a blanket in the front seat of the RSPCB truck. Dr Fielding was driving, and the truck was moving slowly along a country lane. Ulf felt his face: his wolf hair had gone. He licked his teeth: his fangs had receded. He was back to his boy self.

'Ulf, you're awake!' Tiana said from the dashboard.

Dr Fielding glanced over at him. 'Hello, Ulf, did you sleep well?' she asked.

Ulf rubbed his eyes and looked out at the countryside. 'Where are we?' he asked.

'We're nearly home. You've been asleep for hours.'

Tiana sparkled excitedly. 'Oh, Ulf, you were so brave. You saved Howlhammer Castle!'

'Did I?' Ulf tried to remember what had happened, but his last memory was of being at the zombie camp in Howling Forest.

'You transformed, Ulf,' Tiana explained. 'You defeated the Baron and the zombie army.'

Dr Fielding smiled. 'You saved King Stephen too, Sir Ulf.'

'Sir Ulf?' Ulf said, confused. 'Did you call me Sir Ulf?'

'Yes. Sir Ulf the Werewolf,' Dr Fielding said. 'The King asked me to give you this.' She took a scroll from the glove compartment and handed it to him.

Ulf unrolled it.

Dear Ulf,

Thank you for everything. Howlhammer is safe once more. You must come back to visit one day and ride out with me and my knights. It would be our honour to have you among us. From this day forth I bestow on you the Royal Order of Knight of the Realm.

With thanks,

His Royal Highness, King Stephen of Howlhammer

'He's made me a knight!' Ulf said excitedly.

'It's official,' Tiana said. 'Not bad, eh?'

'You earned it, Ulf,' Dr Fielding told him. 'Had it not been for you, Marackai would have destroyed us all.'

Ulf smiled. Knight of the Realm, now that was pretty cool. He rolled up the scroll then looked at Dr Fielding. 'Marackai had the Professor's phoenix all along,' he said. 'He's been using its tears to stay alive. It was his plan to get us to the castle so he could kill us using Harold's army.'

'Tiana's told me everything,' Dr Fielding said. She gave Ulf a look of concern. 'She even told me about the fake moonjuice from the Potions Room. You could have been killed, Ulf.'

Ulf shuddered, remembering drinking the poison.

'You could have ended up like Poisoned Pete, Ulf,' Tiana said.

Ulf remembered the ghosts of Howlhammer. 'Will the ghosts be okay, Dr Fielding?' he asked.

'I believe so. They're all excited to be living again. Zazz will keep an eye on them.'

'And what about the zombies?'

'Take a look behind us, Ulf,' Tiana said.

Ulf leaned out of his window. To his surprise he saw the zombie army jogging behind the truck. They were being led by Orson, hundreds of them stretching down the road as far as he could see. 'Hey, Orson, what are you doing with all those zombies?' Ulf called, waving.

'They're coming to Farraway Hall with us, Ulf,' the giant replied.

The giant had Headless Harold's head in his hand and it was shouting orders, 'Left, right, left, right…'

Tiana perched on the wing mirror. 'Orson says he can use their help around the beast park until we find them a permanent home,' she said.

Ulf felt a long tongue flick down and lick his face. Then he heard Druce's voice singing from the roof of the truck, 'Fur Face knight now, battle won. Stinky zombies run, run, run!'

Ulf smiled. 'That's a nice rhyme, Druce,' he said, wiping spit from his cheek. Then he sat back in his seat as the truck headed south along winding lanes, the zombie army following behind. It wasn't long until the truck turned down the long driveway to Farraway Hall. The gates opened and they pulled up in the yard.

As Ulf got out, Druce leapt over him from the truck's roof and bounded up the side of the house. 'Birdy!' the gargoyle gurgled.

Ulf looked up and saw a golden bird circling above Farraway Hall. It was the Professor's golden phoenix! It swooped then perched on a chimneypot.

'It's followed us!' Tiana said, zooming up to see.

Dr Fielding stepped to Ulf's side. 'This is the first time a Golden Fork-tail phoenix has roosted at Farraway Hall since Professor Farraway's day,' she said. 'If the Professor was alive now he'd be very proud of you, Ulf.'

'Thanks,' Ulf said.

Dr Fielding took her medical bag from the back of the truck, and Ulf followed her to the house. As she stepped into her office and started unpacking, he saw her take out a rack of test tubes containing her samples of golden tears. He had an idea. 'Dr Fielding, may I borrow one of those please?'

'What for, Ulf?'

Ulf took a test tube from the rack. 'Follow me and I'll show you,' he said and he headed upstairs.

Dr Fielding followed him, puzzled. 'Ulf, what are you up to?'

'It's a surprise,' he said, hurrying excitedly along the Gallery of Science then through the Room of Curiosities. He opened the door of the old library and stepped into the gloom. 'Professor, we're back,' he said.

At the far side of the room, beneath a portrait of Professor Farraway, a candle flame flickered on. Ulf walked towards it. 'Dr Fielding, there's someone I'd like you to meet,' he said.

Ulf flicked a few golden droplets into the air around the candle then watched as a hand began forming. It was holding the candlestick. Then an arm began forming, then a body dressed in a tweed suit. Finally, a man's face appeared, his kind eyes twinkling in the darkness. 'Hello, Ulf,' the man said. 'It's so nice to meet you properly at last.'

Dr Fielding stared, stunned. 'Professor Farraway? Is that really you?'

The Professor patted his body and smiled. 'I believe so,' he said. He shook Dr Fielding by the hand. 'I must thank you for doing a marvellous job here at Farraway Hall, Dr Fielding.'

'Professor, your phoenix is back,' Ulf said. 'It's safe now. Marackai got what was coming to him.'

Professor Farraway looked down at Ulf. 'I'm so sorry for the trouble that son of mine has caused you. He's a rotten egg, that one.'

'Professor, he said he'd be back.'

The Professor placed his hand reassuringly on Ulf's shoulder. 'Then we had better put an end to his wickedness once and for all,' he said. 'Now, how about you show me around the beast park while we think of a plan?'

THE END... FOR NOW

**Turn the page for the
first exciting chapters of
*The Big Beast Sale***

CHAPTER ONE

One cold winter's evening, a man in a long fur coat strode along the snowy streets of Capitol City. He turned up his collar to hide his face, his eyes darting left and right at people and cars passing by. At the corner of a dingy side street he glanced behind him and called, 'Blud, Bone, get a move on.'

Two men were following: a small man, Blud, who was dabbing his nose with a red rag, and a big man, Bone, whose beard was frosted with icicles.

'But I'm fr–freezing c–c–cold, B–b–baron Marackai,' the big man Bone said, trudging nearer.

'And I've got the sniffs, Sir,' the small man Blud added.

Baron Marackai glared at them both impatiently. 'Stop complaining, you wimps. There's business to attend to. *This* is where my plan begins.' He brushed the snow from a sign at the entrance to the side street, revealing the words **WILDCAT ALLEY**.

Blud skittered to the Baron's side. 'What plan, Sir?'

'My revenge against the RSPCB, of course! This time I shall finish them once and for all. Now, follow me.' Baron Marackai glanced up and down the street, checking he wasn't being watched, then strode into Wildcat Alley, his serpent-skin boots crunching on its snowy cobbles.

Wildcat Alley seemed deserted. Along its length, on either side, stood shops that looked like they hadn't sold a thing in years: a shabby hat shop, a crusty pie shop, a dusty wig shop, a run-down chemist, a greasy café, a scruffy shoe shop, and shops selling tatty furniture, clothes and ornaments. It was the end of the day and all the shops' signs were now turned to CLOSED.

The Baron stopped at the only shop with its light still on. It was a butcher's and its windows were steamy. He peered in at a crowd of people gathered inside. 'Good. They're here, just as I requested. Keep watch, you two. Don't let anyone else in.'

'Yes, Sir. Whatever you say, Sir,' Blud and Bone replied.

The Baron pushed open the door to the butcher's shop and a bell tinkled, causing the people inside to turn and look at him as he entered. The Baron forced his twisted face into a smile. 'Shopkeepers of Wildcat Alley, how wonderful to see you all,' he said, closing the door behind him and shaking the snow from his fur coat.

'It's been a long time, Baron,' Sam Enema, the butcher, replied. 'What brings you to Capitol City?'

'And why ask for a secret meeting?' Henry

Foxton, the owner of Wildcat Alley's hat shop, added.

'Because I have exciting news for you all,' Baron Marackai replied, surveying the gathering of shopkeepers. 'I know the whereabouts of some very rare beasts! Beasts from which you could make the finest goods to sell in your shops. And they're right here in this city.'

'*Beasts! Here in Capitol City?*' Jemima Fatchuck the pie seller exclaimed.

The Baron nodded. 'And I know how to get my hands on them.'

A ripple of excitement spread among the shopkeepers.

'What kinds of beasts, Baron?' Tony Malone the furniture seller asked.

'All kinds: an impossipus… a slurper…' The Baron edged a step closer, his eyes widening. 'And for a higher price, I could even get you metamorphs too.'

'*Metamorphs!*' The crowd gasped.

'Oh yes, metamorphs: the most elusive

of beasts,' the Baron replied, grinning.

Henry Foxton the hat seller raised a trembling hand. 'But times have changed, Baron Marackai – aren't you forgetting the RSPCB? If they catch us selling beast goods here these days they'll have us arrested,' he said nervously.

But the Baron merely laughed. 'Have faith, Mr Foxton. I have a plan, and by the time I'm through with it *everyone* in this city will despise beasts just as much as we do. People will be queuing up to buy beast goods at your shops and the RSPCB won't be able to do a thing about it!' He stepped among the shopkeepers gesticulating wildly. 'Fellow beast-haters, these shops used to sell the finest beast goods available: troll sausages, yeti-fur jumpers, fairy jam. It's disgraceful that you're now reduced to trying to scrape a living selling common tat. Your ancestors would be ashamed! Do as I say, and Wildcat Alley will be beastly again!'

The shopkeepers conferred, chatting

enthusiastically, excited by the thought of reviving their businesses.

'We can chop 'em!' Sam Enema the butcher said.

'And boil 'em!' Jemima Fatchuck the pie seller said.

'And stitch 'em!' Bettina Scrag the bag seller said.

'Yes, that's more like it!' the Baron told them. 'It's time to prepare your beast mincers, exterminators and extractors; oil your skinning machines and pulpers, get out your beast recipes and cooking pots.' He raised his right hand and wiggled a fleshy stump where his little finger was missing. 'Now, repeat after me: DEATH TO THE RSPCB!'

The shopkeepers raised their right hands and folded down their little fingers. 'Death to the RSPCB!' they repeated. All except Mr Foxton, who was putting on his hat and edging towards the door.

The Baron strode over to him and placed his hand on the hat seller's shoulder. 'Now,

Mr Foxton. You aren't chickening out, are you? Still worried about the RSPCB? Come with me and I will show you a beast that I'm sure will change your mind...'

CHAPTER TWO

The following morning, as dawn broke at the headquarters of the Royal Society for the Prevention of Cruelty to Beasts, Ulf could be found sitting on the snowy roof of his den. He had a book laid open on his lap, and was glancing at it, listening to the sounds of beasts waking across the beast park. From the meat-eater's enclosure he heard the howls of hellhounds, from the Great Grazing Grounds the bellow of a spined armourpod, and from the snowy peak of Sunset Mountain the whistling of mimis. He heard the bulltoxic grunting in the paddock, a magnaturtle warbling in the freshwater lake, griffins cawing in the aviary, and the roar of a yeti from the biodomes. All around the rescue centre, beasts were waking to the day.

A sparkle whizzed towards him from the Dark Forest. It was his best friend Tiana, a woodland fairy. 'Good morning, Ulf. What are you doing up so early?' she asked.

'I'm learning about beast calls from the Professor's book,' Ulf replied. 'It lists more than five hundred different varieties.'

The fairy shook a snowflake from her crocus-petal dress then perched on the book to see. It was *The Book of Beasts*, a notebook containing secrets about every kind of beast imaginable. It had once belonged to Professor Farraway, the world's first cryptozoologist, an expert on rare and endangered beasts.

'Aren't you cold, Ulf?' Tiana asked.

Ulf had on only a T-shirt and jeans, and his bare hairy feet were nestled in the snow. 'I'm fine,' he said. He didn't feel the cold like a normal boy – Ulf was beast blood, a young werewolf who had been brought to the beast rescue centre more than ten years ago when he was just one month old. 'I'm waiting for the Professor,' he said, glancing across the beast park to a figure on a quad bike. 'He's on his way back from feeding the flaming squid in the lagoon. He's promised to teach me how to hatch griffins' eggs.'

At that moment Ulf heard a 'BLURGH!' from behind him and glanced round, recognising the sound. 'Druce, is that you?'

There came a gurgled giggle from behind his den.

'Druce, we know you're there,' Tiana said, darting across the den roof and peeping over its edge.

The ugly face of Druce the gargoyle peered up and his long yellow tongue flicked out, soaking the fairy in spit.

'Eurgh!' Tiana shrieked. 'Druce, stop that!'

'Blurgh!' The gargoyle blew a raspberry at her then scampered away, clambering up a drainpipe on to Farraway Hall, a large country house at the edge of the beast park. Tiana chased after him.

Ulf smiled, watching them play: the fairy trying to blast the gargoyle with her sparkles, and Druce flicking spit at her with his long yellow tongue.

Ulf turned, hearing the *pop pop* of Professor Farraway's quad bike approaching. The Professor was steering the bike with one hand, talking into a walkie-talkie in the other.

Ulf called to him, 'Professor, can we hatch the griffins' eggs now?'

'Sorry, Ulf, I've got to see Dr Fielding in her office straight away,' the Professor called back. 'Something's come up.' And he turned into the yard, heading to the house. *That's odd*, Ulf thought. *It's unlike the Professor not to keep a promise.*

Ulf had spent a great deal of time with Professor Farraway lately, learning about beasts as part of his training to become an RSPCB agent. The Professor was quite a character — more than a hundred years ago he'd founded the RSPCB rescue centre himself. And for the last fifty years he'd even been a beast too: a ghost that had haunted Farraway Hall. Recently, Ulf had sprayed his ghost with phoenix tears, a chemical that could rejuvenate the dead, and now the Professor was enjoying his second human existence.

Ulf slipped *The Book of Beasts* into his shoulder bag, then climbed down from the roof of his den and ran up the side of the paddock to the house, curious to find out what was going on. He was about to head indoors when Orson the giant stepped round from the forecourt, pushing the RSPCB truck.

'Morning, Ulf,' the giant said. 'You might not want to go in there just now. Dr Fielding's in a bit of a fluster.'

Orson was the big beast handler who helped out with the heavy jobs, and Dr Fielding was the RSPCB vet in charge at the centre.

'In a fluster about what?' Ulf asked.

'There's been some kind of trouble,' Orson

replied, pushing the truck across the yard like a wheelbarrow. 'She's asked me to get the truck ready for a mission.' The giant reached into the kit room and pulled out a beast harness.

'What kind of mission?'

The giant shrugged. 'She didn't mention.'

Ulf glanced to Dr Fielding's office window and saw her talking with Professor Farraway inside. Now he was *even more* curious to know what was going on. As Orson loaded the beast harness on to the truck's open back, Ulf called up to Tiana on the rooftop. 'Psst, Tiana, stop chasing Druce and come with me,' he said. 'Something's up.'

The fairy flew down and together they slipped into the house and listened at the door of Dr Fielding's office as she spoke with the Professor inside.

'It's terrible, Professor, it's all over the front page of this morning's newspaper,' Ulf heard Dr Fielding say.

'I'm as shocked as you are,' Professor Farraway replied.

There came the sound of pages being turned.

'What's going on in there?' Tiana whispered.

'I don't know,' Ulf said. He tried peeping through the keyhole, but then footsteps sounded and the door opened.

'I *thought* I heard whispering. What are you two up to?' Dr Fielding said, catching them.

'We were just—'

'Eavesdropping is the word, I think you'll find,' Dr Fielding said. She smiled. 'Well, I suppose you'd better come in and read about it for yourselves.' She pointed to a copy of the *City Gazette* newspaper on her desk. Ulf stepped over and read its front page:

BEAST ATTACK IN CAPITOL CITY!
Report by Dolores Larkin

Citizens today are waking to the realisation that there is a monster in our city – a tentacled beast in City Park lake. Late last night it claimed its first victim. Passers-by saw an as-yet-unidentified man being dragged under the water and eaten alive. The *City Gazette* has contacted the RSPCB for comment, and it appears that the RSPCB was aware of this beast all along...

'There's a beast in the city? In the park lake?' Ulf asked, surprised.

'Yes, an impossipus,' Dr Fielding replied. 'But we hadn't deemed it to be dangerous. It's been living there secretly for years.'

Professor Farraway paced anxiously. 'Why would it suddenly attack?' he muttered. 'It's a good-natured beast. And I've never known an impossipus to eat a human.'

'We're going to have to get it out of the city, and fast,' Dr Fielding explained. 'Not only has a member of the public died, but the reputation of the RSPCB is now on the line too. I've had the reporter from the *City Gazette* on the phone asking why the public hadn't been told about the beast, and now even Major Brigstock of the army too.'

'The army?' Ulf asked.

'Yes. The public are demanding protection. If we don't get that impossipus out of the city at once, the army will open fire on it.'

Ulf gulped anxiously.

'The truck's ready to go,' Orson called from outside. Ulf saw the giant's big face looking in through the office window.

Dr Fielding gave Orson a thumbs up then turned to Professor Farraway. 'Professor, if you can drive to the city and get the beast harnessed, I'll bring the helicopter to airlift it out.'

Professor Farraway nodded. 'I'll leave right away,' he said.

'Can I come?' Ulf asked.

Dr Fielding frowned. 'Hmm, that might not be a good idea, Ulf.'

'But I could help. I'm training to be an RSPCB agent, remember.'

Dr Fielding knelt to face him. 'Ulf, there's more to this than you realise. There are other beasts in the city too, beasts that the public are still unaware of and who absolutely depend on secrecy to live there. You turning up might not be a good idea.'

'Why not?' Ulf asked.

'Because they're metamorphs, Ulf – beasts that look human but can transform. Beasts like you.'

'Like werewolves?'

'Similar, yes: werecats, owl-men, spidrax, froglanoids; and they live among the public without anyone knowing. If a werewolf turned up now, people might start asking more questions, and the metamorphs' cover could be blown.'

Ulf thought for a moment. 'But if I don't tell anyone I'm a werewolf then no one need know.'

Dr Fielding sighed, frustrated by Ulf's stubbornness. 'Well, okay, Ulf. If you promise not to tell anyone you're a werewolf, and to stay with the Professor at all times, I'll let you go.'

'I promise!' Ulf said. 'Brilliant! Thank you, Doctor Fielding.'

Tiana zipped to Dr Fielding's shoulder. 'What about me? Can I go too?'

'You'd better fly with me in the helicopter,' Dr Fielding replied.

The fairy smiled. 'That suits me. I love flying!'

'Then I'll see you there, Tiana,' Ulf told her, and he raced out of the office. 'Hurry, Professor – Capitol City, here we come!'

**Visit www.beastlybusiness.com
for lots of exciting extras
- meet the authors, join the
RSPCB and discover the secrets
of the beasts...!**

SIMON AND SCHUSTER
A CBS Company

BEASTLY BUSINESS

**The Beastly Boys
are David Sinden,
Matthew Morgan and
Guy Macdonald. They met at
school in Kent, and have been
friends ever since.**

SIMON AND SCHUSTER
A CBS Company